"Sebastian, I can't marry you," she said

"I—it was all a mistake," Roxanne continued huskily. "I should never have accepted you—but father wanted that merger."

His hands took her shoulders and made her face him. "You agreed to marry me to make sure the merger went through?"

"Yes," she whispered unhappily. "I never meant to marry you, really. My father was worried sick, and when you asked me... I couldn't see any other way. I'm sorry."

"You're sorry," he repeated. "What comes next? Goodbye, no hard feelings? Or do you hope that we'll always be friends? That might be best, considering your father is now my business partner—or so you imagine. Well, if you expect me to honor that merger, Roxanne, you will damn well honor your promise to me!"

DAPHNE CLAIR
is also the author of these

Harlequin Presents

355—DARLING DECEIVER
367—SOMETHING LESS THAN LOVE
385—A WILDER SHORE
458—DARK REMEMBRANCE

and these

Harlequin Romances

2197—A STREAK OF GOLD
2292—THE SLEEPING FIRE
2392—THE JASMINE BRIDE
2420—NEVER COUNT TOMORROW

DAPHNE CLAIR

promise to pay

Harlequin Books

TORONTO • LONDON • LOS ANGELES • AMSTERDAM
SYDNEY • HAMBURG • PARIS • STOCKHOLM • ATHENS • TOKYO

Harlequin Presents edition published February 1982
ISBN 0-373-10481-2

Original hardcover edition published in 1981
by Mills & Boon Limited

Printed in U.S.A.

CHAPTER ONE

MARK drew up the car at the end of the drive that curved under pepper trees and tamarisks to the front door of Roxanne's home. When he turned to her in the darkness she returned his kiss with fervour, her hair gleaming soft as the moonlight that fell on it as it flowed over his sleeve, her slim body nestling into his arms until she felt him shiver with desire. Gently she tried to disengage herself, then. But his hold tightened and his mouth on hers was desperate, his hands fumbling over her, his breath harsh in her ears.

Distaste suddenly arose in her, and she wrenched away strongly, her voice sharp with anger as she exclaimed, 'Stop it, Mark!'

Still breathing hard, he started the car up the drive, and as she made to get out he said resentfully, 'You led me on—you know you did.'

She didn't answer, because she didn't want a quarrel erupting, but she was furious at the implication. It was a can't win situation, she thought bitterly as she mounted the steps and let herself in, hearing Mark's car roar away down the drive. If she didn't allow kisses at all, she was accused of being frigid, and if she did like a man and enjoy his company well enough to kiss him back, she was 'leading him on'. It was enough to make a girl a man-hater. Certainly at the moment she had had a surfeit of the species.

Her father's study was just inside the front door, and as she turned from closing the door, he came out with another man. She didn't want to meet anyone, had hoped to slip off to her own room without being noticed at all. It was with a sense of exasperated resignation that she returned her father's pleased greeting, and held out a hand to the guest he was introducing to her.

'Sebastian Blair,' he was saying, and something in his voice made her glance sharply at his face as he told the stranger, 'This is my daughter, Roxanne.'

A firm hand clasped hers, and her eyes were drawn from her father's oddly strained expression, to a pair of dark, glinting eyes set in a lean, clever face.

He didn't smile, but the eyes were amused and knowing, and they moved with interest from her rather dishevelled golden-blonde hair to her sapphire blue eyes, jewel-bright with anger, and the full curves of a mouth that had lost its lipstick and still throbbed with the aftermath of Mark's passion.

She had the uncanny feeling that he had guessed with considerable accuracy what had just taken place in the car, and to her distinct annoyance she felt a stinging warmth rise to her cheeks. She almost snatched her hand away, her eyes stormy, and only then the man's mouth, that had remained as uncompromisingly straight as though chiselled in stone, moved into a faint smile.

'I'm very pleased to meet you, Miss Challis,' he murmured. And Roxanne gave him a cool smile and a nod, and said,

'Goodnight, Mr Blair. I'm going to bed, Dad.'

Her father gave her a strange look, and because of it she hesitated for a moment before turning away. It had seemed almost pleading, as though he didn't want her to go—or didn't want to be left alone with his visitor. But that was ridiculous. Her father was a highly successful businessman, and at over fifty he certainly didn't need any hand-holding from his twenty-three-year-old daughter.

The following day was Sunday, and Roxanne accompanied her parents and her younger sister,

Rhonda, to church, helped her mother to serve a leisurely brunch, and planned an afternoon of reading and sunbathing on the patio at the rear of the house. She had donned her briefest bikini and anointed herself copiously with suntan lotion, and was just settling on to a mattress with a thriller when Rhonda called from the house, 'Roxanne! Phone—it's a man.'

'Tell him I'm out,' she answered crossly, sure it was Mark calling to persuade her to forget about last night's tiff.

'What?' Rhonda said.

'Tell him—oh, never mind.'

Reluctantly she got up, the glitter of the sun on the swimming pool hurting her eyes, and the heat baking her bare shoulders as she made her way back to the house across the neatly shorn lawn. 'I suppose I'd better speak to him,' she muttered as she passed her sister.

Her voice probably sounded a trifle curt as she picked up the receiver and said, 'Hello?'

Her hand tightened a little on the cream plastic as the man at the other end asked, 'Is that Roxanne?'

It wasn't Mark. With caution, she acknowledged, 'Yes.' Did she know the voice? She couldn't place it.

'Sebastian Blair,' he said decisively. 'We met last night.'

'Oh. Yes, of course.'

There was a tiny pause. Perhaps he had noted the blank surprise in her voice. He said, 'I'm at a loose end this afternoon. I wondered if you might be, too. Would you like to go for a drive? Perhaps to a beach, for a swim?'

She was staring at the dial on the telephone, still with that feeling of utter surprise. She was accustomed to making an impact; she couldn't help but know that most people thought she was remarkably good-looking, that men often fell quite heavily for her. But she wouldn't have thought she had made that much impression on Sebastian Blair. She had seen no admiration last night in those dark eyes—only appraisal and amusement.

Realising that he was waiting for her answer, she said slowly, 'I'm seldom at a loose end, and we have our own pool for swimming. But thank you for your invitation, Mr Blair. It was kind of you to ask me.'

Again there was a brief pause. Then he said, 'I see. Some other time, perhaps.'

'Perhaps,' she agreed cordially. 'Goodbye, Mr Blair.'

Her father had come out of the lounge and was crossing the hall to his study. He stopped dead as she spoke, and when she put down the receiver, said quickly, 'Blair? Was that Sebastian Blair? What did he want? Why didn't you call me?'

'He asked to speak to me,' she said, with faint amusement now. 'He wanted me to go for a drive with him.'

Owen Challis stared, then looked unmistakably pleased, and Roxanne said gently, 'I turned him down.'

Immediately her father's face changed. For a moment she could have sworn he looked alarmed, then a peculiarly wooden expression came over his features, and he said, 'Well—that's a pity.'

Puzzled, she asked, 'Is he important or something?'

'Yes, he is, rather.'

'Well, if you want me to go out with him——'

Her voice trailed off, because this situation had never arisen before, and she was a little off balance.

For just a moment her father looked eagerly at her, and then he turned away, and in strangely muffled tones said, 'Not if you don't like him, of course. Forget it.'

He went into his study and shut the door, and

Roxanne went back to her mattress and book by the pool, but she couldn't forget the incident. It was too late, anyway, the thing was done. And she had a feeling that Sebastian Blair was not the type of man to lay himself open to a second rebuff, but she wished she had been less hasty. If only her father had hinted to her before the phone call...

Her father rarely discussed his business with his family. Roxanne's mother was a pretty and decorative woman and a charming hostess, but she freely admitted to having no head for business and was content to leave 'all that' to her husband, who had provided her with a very comfortable home and sufficient funds to buy almost anything that took her fancy. His money had seen Roxanne through a university degree in sociology and paid for her and her mother to go on a three-month trip to England and the Continent afterwards. On their return to New Zealand Roxanne had looked for a job that would put her degree to good use, but the one she found, in a government department in Auckland, proved to be little more than glorified clerical work, with scant chance of advancement in an overcrowded field.

Her mother had always wanted her to come home to Waimiro, the thriving town on the tourist route north of Auckland, where her father's company provided work for nearly two hundred people in the TV and stereo assembly plant and the adjacent record pressing plant. He liked to call himself a big fish in a little pond, but the pond was not so small, and his business had expanded to the point where there were other branches scattered about the North Island, and he frequently had to leave Waimiro to check on developments in other parts of the country.

When Roxanne, chafing at the limitations of her job, had come home for Christmas and sighed wistfully over a 'For Sale' notice outside her favourite local craft shop, her mother had taken note. And her father had offered to buy it for her.

'I can't take it with me, or so I've been told,' he said, when she made a protest, and her objections were easily demolished because she really fancied the little shop and the independence and interest it offered.

The shop had been a good investment, bringing in an adequate income, and Bettina Challis had been delighted to have Roxanne living at home again, particularly as Rhonda, now eighteen, was determined on going to art school. Bettina was an affectionate parent, and dreaded the thought of the inevitably empty nest.

This year she had been in her element, with both girls under her wing, but Rhonda was enjoying her long Christmas break now, and in February would be off to Auckland and art school.

Roxanne put down the book which had failed to hold her attention, and turned over on her stomach, loosening her bikini straps to let the sun reach her back. The pool sparkled invitingly, and in the house she could hear her mother singing in snatches as she prepared something complicated for their tea. Bettina was really an exemplary wife. She loved to cook, and although she accepted her daughters' help in the kitchen, she never minded at all if she was left to her own devices there. 'We're spoiled,' Roxanne thought, a trifle guiltily. Some of her friends had been almost scandalised when she told them she was going back home to live. A number of them had struggled for their independence from their parents, and wouldn't have gone back for all the tea in China. But the truth was that after the communal starkness of hostel life, and the friendly chaos of a shared flat, her parents' lovely home and her mother's orderly running of it had a definite appeal. They never interfered in Roxanne's social life, and there were certain advantages in being able to bring home her boy-friends to a discreetly chaperoned situation. Since she had never had any desire to stay the night with any of them, she was usually in at a reasonable hour, and if she expected to be very late for any reason, she would tell her parents so as a matter of common courtesy, but no rules were imposed. It seemed to her an ideal arrangement.

She liked the town, too. It was big enough to supply most things that anyone wanted, and close enough to Auckland to make it an easy trip for shopping or for entertainment. It had one picture theatre and three good licensed restaurants, and was handy to several pretty beaches. Idly, Roxanne wondered which one Sebastian Blair had thought of taking her to this afternoon. Odd, that invitation, after exchanging nothing more than a polite how-do-you-do-and goodnight. Flattering, she admitted, her lips curving in a tiny smile. If she had not been 'off' men at the moment, she supposed she might have accepted.

His face suddenly floated before her vision behind her closed eyes. Dark hair, dark eyes—brown? No, not brown, almost inky blue-black, a strange colour. A face that reminded her vaguely of mediaeval paintings of swarthy, Spanish adventurers. He had been tall, taller than her father by some inches, not thickset but certainly not thin. She hadn't liked him. No, she wouldn't have gone with him—anywhere, even if she had not just had a spat with Mark Fordyce.

Her father had been disappointed, though. Regret stirred briefly. Her father seldom asked anything of her—of any of his family. She would have done it, to please him, if he had given her a hint in time. Troubled, she wondered at his unusual sensitivity to the Blair man. It wasn't like Owen Challis to be anxious to curry favour. He was usually the one on the receiving end . . .

Rhonda flopped down beside her, saying, 'Gosh, you *are* lucky, Rox. Why can't I get a tan like that?'

Roxanne looked up and smiled. Rhonda's skin was very fair, inclined to freckle. Her hair was sandy with faint red lights, thick and with unruly waves. Properly styled and well brushed, it was very attractive, and the tiny freckles that adorned Rhonda's turned-up little nose gave her a certain charm. Roxanne thought her little sister was a very pretty girl, but since she had turned thirteen, Rhonda had anguished over her nose, her freckles, and her fair skin which refused to take on more than the faintest golden colour, and was always threatening to burn and peel.

'The Victorians would have loved your skin,' Roxanne told her. 'You'd have had all the men at your feet, twirling their moustaches and writing poetry to your nose.'

Rhonda giggled. 'I was born out of my time, then,' she said. 'Even the Victorians didn't like freckles, though.'

'Your mama wouldn't have let you get any. You'd have worn those lovely big floppy hats tied under your chin, and carried a parasol everywhere.'

'Oh, I can just see Mum as a Victorian mama! Maybe she's out of her time, too! And I'll tell you who else—that man that was here last night. He doesn't look a bit twentieth century.'

'Funny, I was thinking the same thing just a minute ago,' Roxanne said. 'Mediaeval, isn't he?'

'Did you see him?'

'Only for a minute. How long was he here?'

'Ages. He had a drink with Mum and Dad, and then went off to Dad's study with him to talk business. I think Dad's giving him some advice or something.'

'Do you?' Roxanne was sceptical. She couldn't get out of her mind the fact that her father, for some reason, was terribly anxious to please his guest of last night.

Mark rang just before five, asking her to join him

and some friends for an impromptu beach barbecue. She hesitated, said, 'Just a moment,' and called to her mother, 'Will you mind if I'm not in for tea?'

'Of course not, dear,' Bettina assured her. 'It's only salad and meat loaf.'

Bettina's salads reached a peak of culinary perfection and the finishing touches of tomato roses and radish curls took ages to prepare. The meat loaf would be streets ahead of burnt steaks and sand-dusted sausages washed down with canned drinks. But Roxanne had been restless all day, her mind chewing over the puzzle of her father's attitude to Sebastian Blair, no matter how often she tried to wrench it away. She needed distraction.

'All right,' she said into the receiver. 'What time will you pick me up?'

The beach was still warm from the sun, although the shadows of the pohutukawas that spread silver-clad branches along the shoreline were beginning to lengthen by six o'clock. Some of the trees still held scraps of blood-red starry blossoms, and spent flowers clung among the humps of rough-barked root digging into the sand's edge.

There were five cars, and about twenty or so people in the group. Mark had brought another couple in his car with Roxanne, and they parked on the grass above the beach and unpacked blankets, towels, and containers of food and joined the others who had staked a claim to an area bounded by two pohutukawas, that had several large flat rocks to serve as convenient tables or seats.

Family parties who had enjoyed the beach in the heat of the day were packing up and leaving, and only a solitary fisherman in the distance and a small group with a portable barbecue already smoking several hundred yards away shared the beach with them.

Roxanne greeted several people she knew, and exchanged some laughing remarks with them, keeping herself busy and just out of Mark's reach as he tried to take her hand or put an arm about her waist.

When a deep, steady voice behind her said, 'Hello,' she stiffened with sudden foreknowledge before she turned slowly and met Sebastian Blair's dark, unfathomable eyes.

'Hello, Mr Blair,' she said coolly. 'This is a surprise.'

'It's a small world,' he said, deliberately mocking the triteness of her greeting.

A girl came up to him, tucking a hand into his arm. 'Hello, Roxanne,' she smiled, and behind the smile Roxanne read the message, *This one's mine. Hands off.*

'Hello, Delia,' she said equably, and backed away just a little, a scarcely perceptible movement, but it widened Delia's smile and brought a slight, amused tilt to the corner of Sebastian Blair's mouth.

'Excuse us,' said Delia, tugging at his arm. 'I want you to meet someone, Sebastian.'

Roxanne looked after them as they went, a tall, dark-haired man in light slacks and sandals and a brown cotton shirt open to the waist over a tanned chest, and a small, lusciously formed girl in brief white shorts and and even briefer scarlet top, her blonde hair bouncing on her shoulders as she walked. Roxanne had been at school with Delia Warren when her own hair had been the same shade that it was now, but Delia's had been mid-brown, and she had been plump with puppy fat. After Delia left school she had gone to work in Waimiro's most exclusive hairdressing salon, dieted ferociously and made herself a name as a *femme fatale*. The local girls thought Delia was a bit of a joke, and they watched with varying degrees of irritation and disbelief as she cut a swathe through their menfolk. Occasionally, irritation became downright female fury, when Delia appropriated a male another girl had considered earmarked, but that didn't bother Delia. After years of being a fat, spotty, mouse-haired schoolgirl, now that she had learned how to Make the Best of Herself, she rather enjoyed the reputation of a man-eater.

Sebastian Blair looked well able to take care of himself, anyway, Roxanne thought. She wondered where Delia had found him.

It didn't take long to find out, from snatches of conversation about her. Everyone was curious about the newcomer in their midst. Apparently he was looking about for a house in the district. He had some sort of business in Auckland, but he wanted to live away from the city. Max Ansell, who was in real estate, had been showing him a place earlier today, and asked him along to the barbecue to meet some of the locals. And Max had invited Delia for him. Max himself was escorting a tall, soignée brunette divorcee.

There was a general move towards the water, and Roxanne slipped off the casual slit-sided shift she wore over her white bikini, and allowed Mark to take her hand as they ran into the surf. She pulled free of him as they hit the water, and struck out on her own, heading through the breakers into calm water before she turned and swam in leisurely fashion back to the beach. Delia was fooling daintily about in the shallows, her shorts discarded to reveal a strip of scarlet satin that barely covered her rounded bottom, and several of the men were horsing around in the waves near by, occasionally closing in on her, grinning and splashing. Sebastian Blair wasn't among them.

Roxanne floated about and rode a few breakers in, and then left the water, her hair streaming over her shoulders. Mark materialised beside her, and she gave him an absent smile as they walked back up the sand together. When she saw his hand move towards her, she broke into a run and snatched up her towel, throwing her hair forward to dry it hastily, then swiftly rubbing down her body before tucking the towel about her waist, sarong-fashion.

Max Ansell and another man were arranging a ring of largish stones for the barbecue, and Roxanne said to Mark, 'We'd better earn our supper and find some firewood.'

They were joined by another couple, and strolled along the sand collecting driftwood by the armload, returning with a respectable amount to start off the fire. Roxanne hovered, helping to tend it, and Mark eventually wandered off, a trifle disconsolate, with a group who had volunteered to dig for pipis.

By the time they returned with a bucketful of the tiny shellfish, a grill had been placed over the fire and Max and Roxanne were carefully placing steaks on it, and the other swimmers had left the water and were sitting about in anticipation. Roxanne didn't leave the fire until she had placed two steaks and some salad and bread rolls on two plates, and was able to thrust one into Mark's hand as she sat down beside him.

'Thanks,' he said. 'Enjoying yourself?'

Ignoring the hint of sarcasm in his voice, she said, 'Very much, thanks. How's the steak?'

She wasn't looking at him, her eye had been caught by Sebastian Blair, sitting propped comfortably against a rock on the opposite side of the fire, with Delia kneeling beside him, offering him a plate of pipis that had been boiled over the fire in an old billy can and soused with vinegar. Something in their pose reminded her of an Eastern potentate and a slave girl, and the thought should have been funny, but instead she felt a flash of acute distaste.

She didn't even hear Mark's reply to her question, but he demolished the steak, anyway, and everything else on his plate, and looked more mellow afterwards.

Delia swayed towards them, still wearing nothing but the red bikini, and Roxanne suddenly *was* amused as she saw Mark swallow rather convulsively when the girl leaned over to offer them pipis. Delia must have noticed too; she gave him a come-hither smile before she straightened slowly, passed an appreciative eye over his thick brown curls and deeply tanned chest, and smiled into his almost-goggling blue eyes before she passed on to the next group with her offerings.

Someone had a guitar, and when the food was gone they all moved closer to the fire and joined the guitarist in singing popular songs. Roxanne sat beside Mark and let his arm rest across her bare shoulders. Some of the other girls were sitting within the circle of their boy-friends' arms or half lying against them on the sand. But when Mark moved closer and nuzzled at her neck, she pulled quietly but definitely away.

Sebastian Blair was still propped on the rock, a little out of the circle of the firelight, and Delia was snuggled against him, her hand stroking his thigh, her hair spread against the dark shirt which he still wore. He had an arm about her and his cheek rested against her temple. They looked very intimate for two people who had just met. But to be fair, Delia was like that; Roxanne didn't suppose many men would recoil in outraged virtue from the other girl's rather blatant advances.

The guitarist stopped for a breather, and someone suggested another swim. It was quite dark now, and the pleasant smell of the woodsmoke and outdoor cooking mingled with the sharp odour of the seashore at night. Stars pricked through the velvet cloak of the sky, and the whitecaps on the breakers flashed briefly against the black silk of the mysterious sea.

There was a general movement, and Roxanne shifted away from Mark's restraining arm and got to her feet. She untied the knot on the towel at her waist and dropped it on the ground, and as she looked up saw that Sebastian Blair had come forward into the light of the fire, and was standing on the other side of it—staring at her. He was undressing, slowly pulling off the brown shirt and tossing it behind him. With his eyes on her, dropping over the swell of her breasts to the tautness of her waist and stomach and down her long legs to her feet, his hand went to his belt.

It was ridiculous, everyone was doing the same thing, shedding clothes to reveal the swimming gear they were wearing underneath—this wasn't a skinny-dipping party. But suddenly she felt an unbearable sense of intimacy, as though she and Sebastian Blair were quite alone in someone's bedroom, instead of here on a public beach, in the open air, with umpteen people all around them.

In the darkness she felt hot, and the fire had nothing to do with that: then he raised his eyes, and his belt was undone, and his hand was pulling down the zip of his trousers. He bent to slip them off, and she saw black, clinging swimming trunks, and the curve of his muscled shoulder gleaming darkly red in the firelight, and the black hair like the night behind him.

She swung away quickly and ran down to the sea, leaving Mark behind her, calling her name with plaintive irritation.

She swam far out, much farther than she should have, and floated on her back, looking at the stars and listening to the laughter and squeals of the others as they played about in the breakers nearer the shore.

When a sleek head broke the water near her, she wasn't surprised. There was a kind of inevitability about it. She was surprised, though, when Sebastian Blair spoke, because what he said was, 'What's he done?'

'Who?' she asked blankly.

His arms moved in the water, and he came closer to

her. 'The boy-friend. The one who's getting the cold shoulder from you tonight.'

Icily, she said, 'I don't know what you're talking about.'

'Try again.'

He sounded faintly impatient, and she suddenly flared with irritation herself. She turned over and began to swim away from him, out to sea.

'You're going too far,' he said. 'It's dangerous out here.'

'Don't worry, Mr Blair,' she said, deliberately patronising. 'I swim very well.'

'You don't need to prove it to me,' he said quietly.

He was keeping pace quite easily. She stopped, treading water and trying to see his face. It was too dark, and she said frustratedly, 'If you think I need looking after, you needn't. I told you, I'm very good.'

She thought she caught a faint sound of laughter before he said, 'How good, I wonder?' and suddenly his hands were on her arms, and his limbs wetly entangled with hers in the water as he kissed her.

At the touch of his hands she took a breath, instinctively. His mouth bent her head back, and then they sank beneath the water, into the silent darkness, and she felt the coolness of it all about them, and the salt-tasting warmth of his mouth, the hard body against her softness, his thigh moving gently between hers.

Then they surfaced, and she threshed away from him, panting and gulping in air. She lashed out at him, but found to her chagrin it wasn't possible to slap a man's face while in deep water, and heard him laughing outright.

'Calm down,' he said. 'You'll need all your breath for getting back to the beach.'

It was good advice and, swallowing down her anger, she turned and headed for the shore at a fast crawl.

When she got there he was no longer beside her,

and she staggered up the sand, panting, and collapsed on to a blanket near the dying fire. By the time the others came out of the water, Roxanne had pulled her shift on over her swimsuit, and was sitting hugging her knees and moodily feeding bits of driftwood into the embers. As Mark dropped down beside her she gave him an oblique smile, but her face felt tight, and when he asked if she wanted to go home she said, 'Yes, I'm a bit tired.'

'You swam too far out,' he said chidingly. 'I saw you.'

'You could have come too.'

'I thought you wanted to be alone,' he muttered.

She had, and she had made it obvious. But she hadn't been alone. Sebastian Blair had followed her, all the way. Still, that wasn't Mark's fault, and she touched his hand caressingly, a gesture of contrition.

Eagerly he caught her fingers in his and whispered urgently, 'Forgiven me for last night?'

Roxanne shrugged. 'Of course, Mark.' She liked him; after all, he was a very attractive man, and a decent one. She had never found it hard to respond to his kisses, only last night he had been a bit too pressing. He brushed his lips across her cheek, and she turned deliberately to briefly give him her mouth.

'Let's go,' he said shakily, and she asked, 'What about the other two?'

'Oh, *damn*!' He had forgotten them, and she laughed a little, and said, 'We can't leave them in the lurch.'

'I s'pose not,' he agreed reluctantly, and got up to ask his other passengers if they were ready to leave.

Roxanne sat in the light from the fire, staring at the little tongues of flame flickering about the last few twisted bits of driftwood. A faint, prickling awareness told her she was being watched, but she wouldn't look up. So, Sebastian Blair had probably seen her kissing Mark. It was none of his business what she did. Any more than it was her business that he was sitting over there in the dark with Delia's arms wound around his neck, watching Roxanne over Delia's bottle-blonde head.

CHAPTER TWO

WAIMIRO had a lazy, easy-going air about it that belied the fact of several thriving industries located in the town, the large dairy factory that processed milk from the surrounding farmlands into powdered products for shipping overseas, and the brisk tourist trade from travellers on their way to the historic and proverbially winterless far north. In the town centre there were old shops with the curved corrugated iron verandahs that were traditional for keeping the sun from baking the shoppers and blistering the tar in the pavements; but there were also new stores and offices, gleaming in smart tiles and glass, and two supermarkets stridently advertised their specials in huge red lettering, one at each end of the main street.

Roxanne's craft shop was in a side street that led to the river, a quiet, rippling dark waterway. It had once been the town's lifeline to the world, before the roads came through; taking logs from the kauri and totara forests down to the seaports, and bringing in supplies, settlers and stock for the farms that replaced the great primeval forests as civilisation encroached on the ancient land. Now only pleasure craft occasionally sailed into the town from the sea, anchored at the modest wooden jetty or out in the stream, and provided a talking point for the children who fished from the wharf—barefoot, brown-skinned, healthy little urchins, both Maori and Pakeha. They spent the school holidays splashing in and out of the river, plundering it for its eels and slippery silver fish, diving into its depths from a rock face farther downstream from the wharf, or from the branches of an overhanging puriri, or paddling faded yellow rubber dinghies, smartly painted canoes and ancient rowboats from the town shore to the exciting, bush-tangled stone bank at the other side.

The first week in February, the same little urchins would be sitting at their school desks, washed and neatly dressed, but quite possibly still barefoot until winter came and their mothers persuaded them into shoes and socks.

Roxanne had a helper in the shop, a young married woman with one child who was of school age. Grace Sherwood came in at twelve and stayed until three each day, so that Roxanne could have half an hour for lunch and there were two of them to cope during the usually busiest part of the day.

On fine days Roxanne often took her lunch down to the river and ate sitting on the grassy bank, watching the ducks and the occasional blue heron that frequented it. On the Tuesday after the beach party, she had spent the half hour there and was making her way back to the shop when she saw Sebastian Blair's tall figure going into it.

For a moment she stopped in her tracks, tempted to turn about and lurk in the little park by the river until he had gone. But of course that was silly, and she resolutely quickened her pace instead, and went into the shop herself.

He was talking to Grace, one hand in the pocket of his lightweight grey slacks, the other fingering a small carved box that stood on the counter. Grace was smiling at him, and when Roxanne came in she said, 'Here she is!' and effaced herself swiftly, giving Roxanne a look that said plainly enough, *Lucky you!* as she melted through the curtain that divided their little office-cum-store-room from the shop proper.

'You wanted to see me?' Roxanne asked distantly, her eyebrows raised politely as though she couldn't think of a single reason why he should.

'Your father has asked me to dinner at your place,' he said. 'He thought you might appreciate a lift home, as I'll be going that way.'

'I usually walk,' she said, 'if Dad doesn't pick me up.'

'Yes, so he said. But it's very hot for walking.'

It was, a sweltering January day, and she said, trying to smile naturally at him, 'Yes. Thank you. I finish at five.'

'I'll be here,' he promised. Then he picked up the box and said, 'This is good. Who did it?'

'Mr Ihaka. He's local. There are not many really good Maori carvers about these days.'

'I know.' He inspected the intricate scroll patterns, filled in with tiny symmetrical nicks, and said, 'There's a lot of inferior work turned out for the tourist trade, crude assembly line stuff. You're lucky if you've found a real craftsman.'

'There's some more of his work over here, if you're interested.' She led him to a corner of the shop where more carvings were displayed along with inlaid paua shell work and some turned wooden bowls. She watched as he picked up one or two pieces and studied them. He had good hands, long-fingered and strong, and he handled the things as though he enjoyed the feel of them, running his fingertips over the smoothness of the bowls and the chisel-marks of the carvings with an air of interested absorption.

'I like this,' he said, picking up a shallow bowl that had a band of traditional-style carving decorating it near the rim. 'Is this Mr Ihaka's?'

'It's done by a pupil of his, a girl.'

He seemed surprised, and Roxanne laughed and said, 'She had to wear down considerable resistance. He refused point blank at first to even think of teaching a woman. Even now, there are things he won't let her touch, that he says are *tapu* for a female. He only condescends to teach her because he can't get a boy interested, and she persuaded him the old skills are too valuable not to be passed on.'

'She sounds like a very determined lady.'

'She is. Would you like to meet her?'

'When?'

She had fallen right into that, Roxanne realised. 'I—I'll see what I can arrange,' she said vaguely.

He looked as though he knew she regretted making the offer, but all he said was, 'I'll take this, please.' And she wrapped the bowl for him and took the money with what she hoped was a businesslike air. Other customers came in and he left while she was showing them some pottery jugs.

When she closed the shop, he was waiting outside, and he touched her arm lightly as he guided her to his car, parked just around the corner. It was cool driving with the windows open, and Roxanne sank into the leather upholstery gratefully, and tipped her head a little to allow the breeze to ruffle through her loose hair.

'Did my father ask you to pick me up?' she asked him.

'No. He mentioned that you work in the town, and I offered.'

It sounded as though a broad hint had been dropped, she thought, and again the tiny prick of puzzled doubt assailed her. She couldn't very well ask why her father had invited him to dinner, but she wondered, all the same. Why was it so important to please this man?

She stared at him covertly, watching the lean profile as he drove along the broad main street and turned into the narrow one which wound uphill behind the shopping centre, leading to the houses that overlooked the old town and the river.

'I believe you plan to settle here,' she said. 'Have

you found a place yet?'

'Not definitely. There are one or two possibles.'

'Why do you want to live here?'

'It's pleasant, quiet, close to the city and handy to some of the best beaches around.'

'You don't strike me as a man who likes a quiet life,' she said.

'You don't know me, Roxanne.'

It was the first time he had called her by her name, and the sound of it on his lips gave her an odd little shock. He said it with a strange, deliberate inflection, and for a moment she fleetingly remembered the moment on the beach when he had held her eyes with his as he loosened the buckle on his belt.

It was crazy to blush, but that was what she was doing, and she looked quickly away from him gazing out of the window at her side, hoping that if he noticed, he would put it down to the heat. 'My father knows you, apparently,' she said.

'I only met him this week.'

She glanced at him again, briefly, because that surprised her.

'A mutual friend told me to look him up,' he explained. 'We're more or less in the same line of business.'

'What do you do?' she asked, curious.

'I'm managing director of Renner Electronics.'

Roxanne had heard of them, of course. They were big—bigger even than her father's firm. In some areas she understood that there was some pretty fierce competition between the two. 'I see,' she said. Then, looking at him again, she said, 'Aren't you rather young for that?' He couldn't be more than in his early thirties, she thought.

'Nepotism,' he explained without embarrassment. 'It's a family business. My mother was a Renner.'

She wondered if that meant he simply carried the

title and let other people work while he raked in the resultant shekels. He certainly didn't seem to be working at the moment, staying in the poshest hotel in town while he looked about for a country place to buy. And did this explain her father's attitude?

'You're not planning to set up a branch here, are you?' she asked him.

'Why do you ask that?' he asked.

Because my father is worried by you, and maybe he thinks you're too much competition, she was thinking. *Especially if you're contemplating setting up in his own back yard.* But she couldn't say that. Perhaps she ought to be very careful, here. Her father, for whatever reason, was bent on cultivating the man. She didn't want to upset any plans that Owen Challis might have.

'I just wondered,' she said, with apparent casualness. '*Are* you?'

'I've thought of it,' he admitted.

'And——?'

'No firm decisions yet.'

She wondered if Owen hoped to talk him out of it. Surely there wasn't room for two such similar enterprises in the town? There was a certain amount of unemployment, she knew, but she also knew from remarks of her father's that skilled workers took time to train, and there weren't too many of them around. 'Have you spoken to my father about it?' she asked him.

'Some——' he answered briefly, and then they drew up outside her home, and he leaned over her to open her door.

Her father came out to meet them, and the look he gave her held the same hint of anxious pleading. *Be nice to him,* it said.

Well, she would be, it was the least she could do. While Owen was giving Sebastian a drink in the lounge, she went to her bedroom to change, finding a cool, bare-necked dress in deep blue voile, and scooping up her hair into a knot, leaving a few tantalising, loosely curling tendrils free. A lukewarm shower had freshened her, and she used a light cologne and a touch of mascara, eyeshadow and pink lipstick. She went to offer her mother help in the kitchen, but Bettina sent her away. Rhonda was there obediently slicing salad vegetables and arranging slices of cold meats on their best china. She cast Roxanne a look that said, *What's all the fuss about?* and Roxanne shrugged her own silent, bewildered reply.

The men were sitting in two armchairs when she went in, and for a moment she stood in the doorway, her high-heeled sandals sinking into the deep pile of the carpet. Her father was leaning forward as though making a point, and the other man sat easily in his chair, his long legs casually stretched out before him, crossed at the ankles, his drink held in a loose grasp in one hand.

They saw her, and Sebastian stood up, and for the first time smiled at her. Properly smiled, as though he was pleased to see her, not as though she simply amused him.

'Please sit down, Mr Blair,' she said, and went to the drinks cabinet to pour herself a sherry.

He remained standing, though, until she had seated herself on the sofa, and then he changed his position to sit there, too, taking the other end and half turning to address her. 'I thought we'd got to first names, Roxanne,' he said.

She quelled the urge to retort, *You* might have, and instead gave him a sweet hostess smile and said, 'Sebastian is such a mouthful. Wasn't he the saint who got shot full of arrows?'

'I believe so,' he agreed gravely. 'I should warn you, I'm not available for target practice.'

Her father laughed, but Roxanne looked into the

dark eyes holding hers, and saw that he wasn't deceived by her smile. And he wasn't joking, either.

She sipped her sherry thoughtfully. He was no fool, this man. She would have to tread warily if she was to help her father with whatever it was that he wanted of Sebastian Blair.

She put herself out to be unobtrusively charming for the remainder of the evening. Once or twice she caught a flash of something in the dark eyes that might have been surprise. But he, too, was being perfectly charming. He complimented Bettina on the superb meal, and struck just the right note of friendly teasing to overcome Rhonda's initial shyness with him. He exchanged shrewd comments with Owen on the headline news about export development when they switched on the television to catch the late news, and contrived to convey to them all, without being in the least obvious or embarrassing, that he was very interested in Roxanne.

When he had gone, and she helped her mother to load the coffee cups they had used at supper into the dishwasher, she asked, 'What's so special about Sebastian Blair?'

Her mother laughed rather selfconsciously and said, 'Well, he's very eligible, dear.'

'What?' Roxanne stared. 'You mean—you don't mean Dad is *matchmaking*?'

'Of course not,' her mother said with dignity. 'But naturally as parents we want you to meet the kind of man that—that you might find—acceptable.'

'Did you put Dad up to asking him to dinner?'

'Certainly not. It was your father's own idea entirely. And I must say, he does seem a very nice young man.'

A nice young man was the last description she would have given to Sebastian Blair, but Roxanne didn't say so. 'Actually, I meet plenty of nice young men,' she said.

'Yes, but you haven't exactly—I mean, there's never been anyone *special*, has there, dear? Although I wondered if Mark—still, another string, you know . . .'

'To my bow?' Roxanne finished. 'Are you afraid I'll get left on the shelf?'

'No chance,' said Rhonda, wandering into the kitchen, clad in a cotton nightgown, her nose covered in a white, greasy film that smelled faintly of lemon and garlic. 'Roxanne is definitely not fated to be a spinster.'

'I thought you'd gone to bed,' her mother said severely.

'I'm on my way,' Rhonda replied reassuringly. 'I'm hungry.'

'You'll get fat,' Roxanne warned automatically, as she watched her sister pile butter and cheese and a thick slice of tomato on a piece of bread and bite into it with satisfaction. 'What on earth is that you've got on your nose?'

'Freckle cream. Got it at that health food and organic remedies place near your shop.'

'Cucumber,' their mother murmured, and two pairs of eyes swivelled to her in fascinated enquiry. 'Cucumber lotion,' she explained. 'It was used for freckles in the nineteenth century, I think.'

Bemused by their reaction, she left both her daughters convulsed with laughter, and went to seek her husband's assurance that the evening had gone very well, and the dinner had been up to her usual standard.

Roxanne went to bed and slept well, but at some dark hour of the morning she woke on the sudden clear and unmistakable thought that her father, at least, was no matchmaker. If he had let her mother think that was his motive for encouraging Sebastian Blair, it was only a cover for something else that he had on his mind.

Something that he didn't want to burden his wife with.

Roxanne's father usually dropped her off at the shop on the way to his office. This morning she looked at his preoccupied profile and said, 'Dad, what's so important about Sebastian Blair?'

He changed gear as the car ran into the long, winding road down the hill, and said, 'Important?'

'You said he was rather important,' she reminded him. 'And you're going to some trouble to—to keep him sweet, aren't you?'

Her father flushed, making her stare in surprise. 'One dinner isn't a lot of trouble,' he said shortly. 'He's the top man in Renner Electronics, and it's only common courtesy to make him welcome, since he apparently plans to live in Waimiro.'

'I see. Mum had the idea you thought he'd make me a good husband.'

She gave him a sidelong grin, but he didn't smile back. He looked uncomfortable, and muttered, 'Your mother gets some odd ideas into her head sometimes.'

Yes, she thought grimly. *Especially when you put them there.*

'All the same,' he added, 'he would certainly be very—very acceptable, if he—if you——Well, you never know.'

Testing, she said deliberately, 'Actually, I don't like him, much. Does it matter?'

'No, of course not.' But the hollow note in his voice betrayed his disappointment, and the frown on his forehead deepened. He drove in silence the rest of the way to the shop, but as she gathered up her bag and made to get out, he said suddenly, 'Roxanne!' And when she turned in surprise, went on, 'You won't—do anything to antagonise Sebastian, will you? I—er—would rather not have any awkwardness there.'

Gently she said, 'Daddy, what do you want me to do?'

He drew back. 'Nothing,' he said harshly. 'I'm not asking you to do anything that goes against the grain. Only Sebastian likes you, and the situation is a bit—well, a bit awkward. Just be—tactful, please, there's a good girl.'

'Yes, of course,' she promised. 'But I wish you'd tell me the real reason. You're worried, I know you are. Please, Dad—I'm not a baby, you know.'

He ran a harassed hand over his thinning hair and looked at her measuringly. 'All right,' he said finally. 'But not a word to your mother or Rhonda—promise?'

'Of course I do.'

He took a deep breath, his hands gripping the wheel in front of him. 'The fact is,' he confessed, 'the firm is in trouble. I was beginning to wonder how much longer we could go on like this, I would have had to think about selling out. Sebastian doesn't know this, but if he opened a branch of Renners here I think it would finish me. On the other hand, if I could persuade him into a merger it would save us.'

'If you had to sell out,' Roxanne asked, hushed, 'how bad would it be? I mean, there'd be money—surely?'

He shook his head. 'I'm mortgaged up to my ears. The house would have to go. Rhonda's art school——' he shrugged, 'well, I'd try to manage that somehow.'

Roxanne felt slightly dizzy with the shock of it. Her mother's lovely home that she lavished such care and attention on, the house filled with furniture, paintings, ornaments, that had been specially chosen for the comfort and pleasure of her family; her super-efficient kitchen where she spent so many hours happily planning and perfecting the meals that she loved to concoct; the garden where every tree and shrub and bulb had been planted by Bettina herself, and watched over almost as anxiously as her children had been as they grew. And Rhonda, perhaps deprived of her ambition, having to go into an office or shop, when all she longed to do was tied up in art.

'I'll do anything I can to help,' she assured her father.

'Now don't get carried away,' he warned. 'There's no need to be thinking of dramatic sacrifices, my dear. It's not the end of the world.'

'Okay,' she said, giving him a shaky smile. 'I'll try not to rock the boat, though.'

He patted her hand awkwardly and said, 'Good girl.'

Well, at least she knew now, Roxanne thought as she unlocked the door of the shop. Of course it wasn't the end of the world. But it was worse than she had ever thought it could be.

There was one thing she could do. She made a couple of phone calls and then tried to contact Sebastian at his hotel. He was out, so she left a message, and early in the afternoon he rang back.

'You wanted me?' he said, his voice softly intrigued.

'The lady you wanted to meet,' she said coolly. 'If you're still interested, she's free after five today.'

'Oh, I'm interested,' he said, still in that provocative tone. 'Shall I pick you up? You *are* going to introduce me, aren't you?'

'If you like. I'll see you later, then.'

'Thank you,' he said.

'That's all right. Goodbye.'

She might have been a bit more—gracious, she supposed. The trouble was, something about him made her prickle all over, an uncomfortable feeling. Oh well, if she suddenly changed her tune and was all over him, he'd probably suspect an ulterior motive anyway. A gradual thaw should be much better tactics.

'You're going to meet Mr Ihaka, too,' she told him as

he saw her into his car, later. 'We'll go to his house.'

'Good,' he said. 'Tell me how to get there.'

It was out of the town a little, on a rough, unsealed road, and Mr Ihaka's 'studio' was a large corrugated iron garage at the rear of his shabby little house. Roxanne watched Sebastian talking to the old man, his obvious interest mixed with a hint of deference. The apprentice carver, Herena Kahi, was shy at first, and Roxanne saw the intrigued look on his face as Sebastian looked from the olive-skinned, serene face of the girl to the slightly dour old man who was bullying her into showing their visitor how to carve the *pitau*, or spiral pattern, so typical of Maori art.

He questioned the girl quietly, and after an hour or so he had her talking animatedly, explaining her interest in carving and her long campaign to get Mr Ihaka to teach her. The master carver now and then interrupted with an abrupt comment in English or Maori, and Herena would bow her head as she listened, then flash him a smile and continue talking, her dark eyes sparkling. Then Mr Ihaka took over the conversation, describing the ancient *tapus* associated with the carving of meeting houses and the great war canoes, and how the spiral patterns had been seen in nature, in spiderwebs and the tightly curled immature shoots of the ponga tree ferns that abounded in the native forests, and translated into carvings; or, in the old days, into the *moko* tattooed on the cheeks of the warriors, and the lips and chins of the Maori women. As he talked, he began to stride up and down in the manner of the Maori orator on the *marae*, occasionally waving a chisel to demonstrate a point.

Sebastian bought a small, carved feather-box inlaid with paua shell before they left, and in the car he handed it to Roxanne, saying, 'It's for you. I don't suppose you wear huia feathers, but perhaps you can find something to put in it.'

'I can't——'

'A thank-you,' he interrupted. 'For an enjoyable couple of hours. He's a fascinating old fellow, isn't he?'

'Yes. I'm glad——'

'And Herena is a bit of surprise.'

'Did you expect a muscle-bound young *wahine*?'

'I expected a rather assertive young woman,' he admitted, smiling slightly.

'I take it the surprise was a pleasant one. She's pretty, isn't she?'

'And delightfully submissive.'

'I thought she would appeal to you.'

He gave her a sharp glance. 'You've got me taped as a male chauvinist, haven't you?'

'Do you deny it?'

'I wonder where you get your prejudices from.'

'I'm not prejudiced,' Roxanne declared.

'All right—prove it. Let me give you dinner at my hotel.'

'What will that prove?' she demanded.

'That you're neither prejudiced against me, nor—frightened.'

'Frightened?' She turned quickly to look at him.

'You ran—or rather, *swam* away from me pretty fast the other night,' he reminded her.

'I wasn't frightened,' she said coldly. 'I was furious.'

He looked at her again, consideringly. 'Would the boy-friend have objected?' he asked.

'*I* objected. I don't like being grabbed and kissed against my will.'

'One doesn't usually ask permission to kiss a girl.'

'Most men at least wait for a sign that she would welcome it.'

'I had the impression,' he said, 'that you'd given me one.'

That odd moment of intimacy by the firelight. Remembering, Roxanne felt her face burn. 'You were mistaken,' she said stiffly.

'Was I?' he murmured, and there was scepticism in his look, this time. But he didn't give her a chance to retort. 'Let me make up for it, then,' he suggested. 'A drink and dinner, and then I'll drive you home.'

About to refuse, she paused, recalling that his goodwill was essential to her father. 'All right,' she said, giving in. 'Thank you.'

She phoned home from the hotel, to let her mother know she would be later than she had expected because Sebastian was giving her a meal. Her mother sounded delighted, and Roxanne thought wryly that when she relayed the news to her father he was going to be pleased, too.

The dinner was very enjoyable, Sebastian's conversation was informative and stimulating and frequently amusing, and she found herself falling under the spell of his considerable charm. Reared in the city himself, he expressed curiosity about what it was like to grow up in a country town, and she kept him interested and made him laugh once or twice with anecdotes of her childhood.

He had a very attractive laugh, soft and deep, and it creased his cheeks and softened the bold lines of his face. No wonder Delia had been delighted to be paired off with him the other night, Roxanne thought dispassionately.

When he drove her home, he got out of the car and took her to the front door of the house. She was holding the feather-box, and said, 'Thank you very much, for the dinner, and this.'

'My pleasure,' he said, and tipped her chin with one finger, to press a brief, firm kiss on her lips.

She expected him to go, then. She had her hand on the key that had had been left in the door for her, when he turned her back to face him, his hand on her arm.

'How serious is it, with the boy-friend?' he said.

She wanted to say that it was none of his business, but the thought of her father's problems restrained her. 'I like Mark very much,' she said.

'Is he in love with you?'

'That isn't a fair question.'

His mouth quirked a little. 'Okay. Do you like *me*, Roxanne?'

'I—don't know you very well, do I?' she said evasively.

'You're going to.'

She thought that perhaps she should be a little more forthcoming. She looked up at him, and smiled with slight but deliberate provocation. 'Am I?' she said softly.

Sebastian's eyes narrowed a little. 'Oh, yes.' He bent his head, and she didn't try to avoid him. The kiss this time was longer, his mouth caressing hers with purpose, while his hand held her nape, long fingers stroking the sensitive skin.

She wasn't responding, but she didn't object, either, and when he moved away at last, releasing her, she saw the flash of satisfaction in his eyes, and quickly veiled hers.

'Goodnight, Sebastian,' she said, and slipped into the house before he had time to answer.

CHAPTER THREE

THEY were together a lot in the next few weeks. Sebastian drove her home quite often, stayed for a meal now and then, and sometimes took her to a film or off into the hills or along the coast for a quiet, leisurely drive. She accepted all his invitations, unless she was genuinely engaged elsewhere, and she saw how her father's acute anxiety receded, the gratitude in his eyes as he watched her go off smiling somewhere with Sebastian. Her mother's approval was patent, and even Rhonda confided once that really, Sebastian was 'a bit of all right,' wasn't he?

The only one who didn't approve was Mark. He had been starting to think of Roxanne as his, and perhaps it was as well to break the pattern, because she hadn't been nearly ready for a commitment, and at least her outings with Sebastian made it clear to him that he couldn't take anything for granted. He ran through the gamut of jealousy, hurt and sullen acceptance, and when she met them all with the same serene indifference, stormed off in a huff and didn't contact her for days.

Sebastian had decided on a house. It wasn't in the town itself, but close to a nearby beach, perched on a steep hill overlooking the sea. It was only a few years old, built with wide windows to take advantage of the view and a stone-flagged terrace outside reached through sliding glass doors from the lounge. There were only three other houses near by, and they were screened from sight by native trees which had been left by the landscapers to provide privacy, and a few flowering shrubs gave exotic colour. From the terrace a short flight of steps led to a small lawn bordered with hibiscus and pink and red manuka, and from there a narrow, steep pathway descended to the beach, which was public, but seldom crowded as there was no public access by car, only a half mile walkway from the main road.

He took the whole Challis family to see it one Sunday, while it was empty, and they looked through the cool, airy rooms and had a dip in the sea, and Bettina enjoyed herself giving him advice on furnishing the place.

A few days later, Sebastian took Roxanne out there alone. 'I've been buying furniture,' he said casually. 'Come and tell me that you approve.'

'It's my mother who's the expert,' she demurred, not seriously, a faint smile on her lips.

He was studying her mouth, as he said, 'It's you I want.'

That might mean a number of things. Sidestepping the possible implications, she said, 'Supposing I don't like your choice of furnishings?'

'Then I'll change it.'

'I'll bet!' She didn't believe him, of course. He hadn't meant her to. Ever since they had first met, he had pursued her in a casual way, but it didn't mean he would change anything of his for her sake. Their relationship had not gone deep, Sebastian showed no signs of wanting anything more than a pleasant flirtation, spiced with a few kisses, and Roxanne had been very willing to keep it on that safe and sensible level. She didn't mind him kissing her, he did it with considerable finesse and expertise, and he was a very good-looking man. She would scarcely have been human if she had not enjoyed it. She submitted without demur when he took her in his arms, and felt a definite satisfaction in his unmistakable pleasure in the taste of her mouth, and the contours of her body. And he didn't seem to mind that she was passive rather than responsive to his lovemaking.

He had bought a long sofa and two deep chairs that looked comfortable and smart, and their dark-and-light brown stripes blended with the oatmeal of the curtains that had come with the house. A dark brown shaggy rug was on the floor between them, and there were two smoked glass side tables by the chairs.

One of the two bedrooms had been furnished with a wide bed covered with a plain black silky-looking spread, and two stark white rugs lent a contrasting note against the dark wood floor and matching dark cupboards and drawers. Roxanne stood in the doorway and said, 'It looks very—stylish.'

She turned away then, back to the living room down the short passageway, and asked, 'Have you stocked up your kitchen yet?'

'Hungry?' he said, coming behind her.

They had already eaten, back at her place, and she said, 'No. But I could do with a cool drink.'

'I can provide that.' He took her into the small kitchen and opened a neat, compact refrigerator that stood under one of the counters. He extracted a tall green bottle and took two long-stemmed glasses from a cupboard.

Roxanne watched him pouring the wine with practised, economical movements, and as he handed one to her she raised her brows a little and said, 'Sparkling wine?' The refrigerator had been virtually empty, otherwise. 'This is the first thing you stock up on?' she asked him, only half teasing. Her eyes commented, *So that's the kind of man you are!*

His smile, urbane, careless, and knowing, acknowledged the unspoken comment. 'I wanted to celebrate,' he said. 'I intend to sleep here tonight. It will be the first time.'

Something tightened inside her. The atmosphere

had suddenly, subtly changed. His eyes held hers, darkly compelling, and it was an effort to look away from him and sip at her wine, as though she had noticed no undercurrents, no possible shadows of other meanings in his simple statement.

The kitchen was too small, and she turned without hurry to go into the lounge, standing before the window, pretending to admire the sweep of the hillside with its tree ferns and manuka and tall red flax, and the broad Pacific beyond, throwing white-edged breakers on to the shore.

She finished the wine slowly, and he took her glass, holding his own empty one, and said, 'Another?'

'No, thanks. Let's walk down on the beach. It's so nice and cool out there.'

'Okay. Want to swim?'

Roxanne shook her head. She had brought no swimming gear, was wearing a light, full-skirted summer frock and sandals. It crossed her mind that maybe Sebastian was the kind of man to stock up on spare bikinis, too, and she turned away from him and was out on the flagged terrace before he had put down their glasses.

His long stride soon caught up with her, and they went down the path between the trees in silence. It was still light, and gulls called plaintively to each other over the breakers, even as the crickets began a tentative, soft series of songs close by. Pink, frilly hibiscus from a bush near the edge of the garden had been blown on to the path, and the woody, sharp scent of the manuka mingled with the salty tang of the sea. Sebastian was wearing rope-soled canvas shoes with his casual light slacks and open shirt, and the soft sound of his footfalls behind her made her think of a stalking animal, so that involuntarily she cast a swift, wary glance over her shoulder, and in consequence stumbled as her foot hit a root on the rough path.

Sebastian lunged to catch her, his fingers biting into her arm with unexpected strength as she steadied herself against his arm.

'Careful!' he said sharply.

'Yes, sorry,' she said, easing herself away from him. 'Thanks.'

They reached the soft, cooling sand, in the shadows of the tangled kowhai, korokio and manuka, and walked near the edge of the water, still warmed by the dying rays of the sun.

They strolled to where the sand gave way to a mass of weathered boulders, fallen long ago from the white stone cliffs that thrust up in overhanging folds and pillars from the beach, and walked over and between them, the wind catching at Roxanne's hair and skirt, and flapping at Sebastian's shirt. Their feet splashed through shallow rock pools, avoiding tiny blue starfish and hermit crabs. Sebastian pulled her up finally on to a flat outcrop of rock, and they sat there side by side as the breakers flung against it below them and dewed their faces with fine salt spray.

The daylight faded and the sky turned pale, faintly pink and then shot with green and darkening into purple. The sea became deeply green and then strangely colourless and finally merged with the smudged bluish purple on the skyline, and Sebastian touched her arm as she shivered, running his fingers over the tiny raised goose-pimples on her arm, and said, 'It's cold. Let's go.'

He held her hand as they negotiated the rocks again, and when they neared the pathway, he stopped in the shadow of the overhanging trees and drew her into his arms.

Immediately she sensed a different quality in his embrace, a purposefulness that had never been there before. And she trembled. Perhaps he thought she was still cold, for his arms tightened, and she felt his hand moving again over her upper arm in a warming caress.

Then he was holding her closely, kissing her softly, gently prising her lips apart with his, tipping back her head into the crook of his arm, one hand shaping her shoulder in long, exploring fingers.

He raised his head, and murmured her name, and she made a tentative movement away from him, but his arms tightened again, and he said softly, 'Roxanne,' and brought his lips down to hers again, insistently this time, with a passion that demanded response.

She didn't give it, only staying quiescent in his arms, until he suddenly swung her off her feet and brought her down on to the cool nightwashed sand. She struggled then, trying to push against him as he held her, his body over hers, not heavy but inescapable. And he said softly, 'No. No, it's all right, don't fight me.'

Her hands were pinned against his chest, resisting him, and her body was rigid against the seduction of his. But her panic subsided at the sound of his voice. It was so quiet, so controlled, she realised there was no need for fear.

He kissed her again, with the same urgent but patient persistence, and by almost imperceptible degrees she relaxed, allowing him a bold exploration of her mouth with his, lying quiet and submissive under the increasing heat of his body.

He raised his head and took a long, shuddering breath. His hand found one of hers and he kissed it, hard and hotly, and placed it on his neck. 'Hold me,' he muttered. 'Kiss me back, Roxanne.'

She let her hand slip from the warm, damp flesh to the shoulder of his shirt, and gave an infinitesimal shake of her head.

'*Roxanne!*' he almost groaned it, an angry plea, then his mouth was on hers again, and there was no more gentleness and no more patience. Her hand flattened against his shoulder, her body arching in a desperate effort at escape, and when he refused her any leeway, she dug her nails into his flesh, trying to hurt, but with no effect. His mouth ravaged hers until she stopped resisting him, and then, with devastating suddenness, the kiss changed to a slow, sweet, irresistible seduction of the senses. His fingertips touched her cheek and neck, and slid down her arm and then barely skimmed her breast before coming to rest at her throat, feeling the jumping little pulse-beat that betrayed her agitation. Her bruised lips slowly opened to the persuasive movement of his mouth, and trickles of fire began to flow over her skin, in spite of the cool night air.

He lifted his mouth from hers, and she saw the stars swimming overhead and heard the pounding of the waves. She quivered as he buried his mouth in the soft skin at the curve of her neck and shoulder, and his lips moved lower to find an even softer flesh below. She gave a gasp of surprised pleasure, and her hands went up to hold his head, her fingers tangling in the thick softness of his hair, her body afire with nameless longing.

Sebastian made a sound, too, deep in his throat, inarticulate but explicit, and his mouth came back to hers, sure and devastatingly sensual. At last she put her arms about him, her hands spread and stroking his shoulders, as she arched her throat and kissed him back with passion.

Her eyes closed against the night, she yet could see the stars, for they floated behind her eyelids, and the sea was beating to the shore within her pounding heart. The kiss was going to go on for ever, she thought confusedly—but then he shifted his mouth from hers a little and whispered, 'Roxanne, come back to the house with me.'

She knew exactly what he meant, of course. And to her everlasting shame, it seemed like minutes before she gathered the strength to say, 'No.'

She heard his breath stop, and then he sighed. She felt his muscles tighten, then he moved away from her a little, and the cold breeze on her body made her shiver. He was lying on the sand beside her, his arm still across her body, his hand warmly clasping her shoulder.

'No,' he repeated. His voice held chagrin and resignation, and a hint of grim humour. He raised himself on his elbow, looking down at her, the pale blur of her face in the darkness turned from him, and then he gave a whispered little laugh and said, 'That's it, then.'

He stood up and pulled her to her feet, and all the way up the darkened path he held her hand, but it was an impersonal clasp now, and when they reached the top he released her, retaining only a light touch on her elbow to guide her to the waiting car.

They were nearly back at her home when he said, 'I won't be here at the weekend, I'm going to Auckland for a few days.'

Roxanne didn't reply, unable to think of any comment to make. What could she say? *I'll miss you?* She felt only relief. This was Wednesday. She knew he wouldn't contact her again before the weekend. And after . . .?

She wondered if she had just ruined her father's chance of saving the business. But he had emphatically told her not to make unreasonable sacrifices. What she found shattering was the knowledge that it would have been no sacrifice at all, tonight, to return with Sebastian to the darkened house and the wide, silk-covered bed.

Mark phoned on Saturday afternoon, to ask with an elaborately casual air if she was interested in going to a party being held at Max's place. Roxanne's first instinct was to say no, but she had regretted the rift with Mark. After all, she had always liked him and enjoyed going out with him before Sebastian came along. His jealousy was perhaps natural, although irritating, and if she turned him down now he would almost certainly not come back for more. She said yes, wondering if he had known somehow that Sebastian was away.

The usual crowd was at the party, and Mark seemed to be putting himself out to be his old self, confident, charming, and a very pleasant escort for an evening's entertainment.

One of the men asked, 'Where's the divine Delia tonight?' and amid a good deal of winking and leering, someone else said she was away for the weekend.

'I tried to get hold of her,' Max explained. 'But I'm told she left the salon on the dot of five yesterday, picked up by Sebastian Blair in person, and he stowed her little suitcase into the trunk of his car right alongside his own, then took off into the wild blue yonder.'

There were one or two knowing hoots, and some laughter, and one of the girls made a feline comment under her breath, but Delia was popular among the men, who thought of her as a good sort but seldom displayed much jealousy over her roving blue eyes, and Sebastian was obviously a fairly prominent feather in her cap. The general feeling was one of mild, good-natured envy, and good luck to them both.

Roxanne, who had turned cold and then burningly hot, realised that Mark was regarding her with a fixed, intent stare. She turned a dazzling smile on him and said, 'Penny for them?' She was damned well not going to let *anyone* guess that the news had rocked her with an inexplicable anger and distaste. Later, she rationalised that to herself as a quite understandable reaction. Sebastian had been making fairly passionate love to herself only two days before taking off for a weekend with Delia, after all. He might possibly have invited *her* along for the ride, if she had been more amenable—or stupid—that night. She couldn't help remembering that he had accepted her refusal rather philosophically. Because apparently it hadn't mattered too much which girl he took with him, and Delia—*Delia!*—was an adequate substitute.

No wonder Roxanne was quietly seething, but meantime she put a convincing act on of enjoying the party, drank a good deal of Max's liquor, and danced and sang and laughed and flirted amicably with Mark and one or two others until two o'clock in the morning.

Mark's kiss outside her door was circumspect, and she was grateful for that. A tussle in the dark was the last thing she needed right now. In the morning, sitting heavy-eyed in church beside her mother, she repented the drink. It hadn't done much good at the time, except to lend a sparkle to her eyes and a certain recklessness to her bitter mood, and now she was feeling the retribution in a hammering at her temples and a slightly nauseated feeling in her stomach. She hadn't been drunk by any means, but she had certainly consumed more than was good for her. Damn Sebastian Blair, she thought dispassionately, and then, recalling her surroundings, begged silently if not entirely sincerely for forgiveness, and tried to concentrate on the sermon.

By the end of the week, Roxanne had heard at third hand the news that Delia had returned to work on Monday morning looking like a cat that had been surfeited on cream, and dropping casual remarks to her friends about Sebastian's car, Sebastian's driving—and Sebastian's flat, as well as Sebastian's admiring remarks about herself. 'He's got a thing about leather, Delia says,' Roxanne's informant asserted, and for a moment Roxanne's mind boggled. 'Couches, chairs,' the girl added. 'Not vinyl, Delia reckons, the real thing.

You know, it costs the earth. But then he's loaded, isn't he? Black, Delia said. The couches.'

'Yes,' Roxanne said. 'He likes black.' She had a fleeting image of Delia's pale hair against a high-backed leather couch, her preposterously lengthened and blackened eyelashes lowered provocatively, legs crossed so that her skirt rode just a little above the knee . . .

'Does he?' The informant was suddenly avid, waiting breathlessly for Roxanne's next words, having suddenly remembered, obviously, that Sebastian had sometimes been seen about with Roxanne, after all . . .

For a mad moment she was tempted to describe the bed in his house, and add that he had invited her to share it with him. *That* might give Delia something to think about, when she heard of it, she reckoned, and pulled herself up sharply. Since when was *she* engaged in a cheap contest with Delia Warren? Or with anyone, for that matter. Sebastian Blair was just a man who had kissed her a few times, who had once managed to rouse a purely instinctive, perfectly natural response simply because he was apparently some kind of expert at that sort of thing. And from the first she had tolerated his company only for her family's sake.

'Mm,' she murmured, as noncommittally as possible, and deftly turned the conversation into other channels. At least, at the time she thought it was deft. Afterwards she wondered if she had been allowed to do so on the grounds of compassion for a woman scorned. The possibility made her squirm.

She asked her father on Friday morning, 'Have you heard from Sebastian since he came back?'

'Has he been away?' He looked faintly relieved. 'Wondered why we hadn't seen him around lately.'

He had wondered if she had done something to drive Sebastian away. But he hadn't asked. It must have cost him, she thought. Now he was convinced everything was all right, and what if it wasn't?

Carefully, she said, 'Well, he's been in Auckland, but we might not see him so much. The word is that he's—er—interested in Delia Warren. Apparently he took her with him.'

'Delia?' Her father gave her a sidelong, incredulous smile. 'Even if it's true, I can't see it lasting long.'

No, it probably wouldn't; Delia was like a pretty, insubstantial butterfly, flitting from one conquest to the next. But this could last long enough to put paid to her father's plans, all the same. And anyway, even with her father's business at stake, Roxanne wasn't going to cool her heels while Sebastian transferred his attentions, however temporarily, and welcome him with open arms when he finally condescended to remember her existence . . .

But that night it was Sebastian who was waiting for her outside the shop when she locked up after the late closing time.

'I'm expecting my father,' she said coolly.

Sebastian smiled. 'I know. But I offered to pick you up and save him the trip.'

'Thank you.' She managed a perfunctory smile, then avoided his eyes as they walked to the car and he opened the door for her.

When he slid into the driver's seat, he said, 'Can I give you supper, before I drive you home?'

'No, thank you,' she said distantly. 'I'm tired.'

She felt his quick, probing glance, but wouldn't return it. He said, 'Okay. Home it is.'

He asked her how business was, and she said, fine. She could have asked, 'How was the trip to Auckland?' because she hadn't seen him since. Instead, she talked at random about stock turnovers and peak selling periods, until they reached her house.

Sebastian got out and opened the door for her, then

waited for her to ask him in. She was tempted to say thanks and goodbye, but her father knew that he was bringing her home, and in the end she said, 'Dad will be expecting you. Please come in.'

She thought his mouth tightened a little, but there was very little light, and he only said, 'Thank you. He did say he'd like to see me.'

Owen's greeting was just short of effusive, and Bettina made coffee and served it with tiny biscuits piped with cream cheese and garnished with tomatoes and gherkins, and slices of cream-filled chocolate cake. Roxanne nearly spilled her coffee when Sebastian mentioned that he had only returned today from Auckland, and he glanced at her with brows raised, meeting her surprised stare with a suddenly narrowed gaze before he turned back to continue speaking to her father.

After one or two abortive attempts to draw her into the conversation, Owen had given up, and devoted his attention to Sebastian. Sebastian didn't look her way again, but when she stood up and said, 'I'm tired. If you'll all excuse me, I'll go to bed,' he stood up, too.

'See me out first,' he said, smiling. 'I could do with an early night myself.'

Briefly her fingers curled into her palms, but she caught her father's eager look, and managed to accompany Sebastian to the door with something approaching politeness. He took her arm there and compelled her out on to the driveway with him, turning to face her as they reached his car.

'What was the big surprise about my arriving today?' he demanded.

'I don't know what you mean.'

'Yes, you do. You nearly choked when I mentioned it.' He paused, looking down at her averted head. 'Is that the reason for the cold shoulder?' he asked slowly. 'You thought I'd have been back earlier, and I hadn't contacted you? Is that it?'

'Of course not. What you do with your time is your own business.'

'I wish you'd tell me.' His voice was low and almost coaxing, and she hated him—*hated* him.

'There's nothing to tell,' she shrugged, and made to turn away. But his hand caught her wrist firmly, stopping her.

'Are you upset about what happened last week, before I went away?' he asked her. 'I hope you're not expecting me to apologise, Roxanne. I couldn't sincerely say I'm sorry. I enjoyed it.' Again he paused. Then he said deliberately, 'And so did you. I'm only sorry you didn't want to take it any farther.'

Roxanne jerked her wrist from his hold, and said furiously, 'Well, it didn't take you long to find someone more accommodating, did it?'

'*What?*' His voice was like a pistol shot, making her wince.

'You didn't think it was a *secret*, did you?' she said. 'You'll have to get used to living in a small town, Sebastian. It's common knowledge that Delia went to Auckland with you.'

His silence had an oddly blank quality. Then he said, 'Yes, she did. So what?'

Trying to sound calm and unconcerned, she said, 'So I was naturally surprised that you hadn't returned when she did, that's all.'

A trifle grimly, he said, 'But that's *not* all, is it? You—the whole town, I suppose—jumped to conclusions, simply because I gave a girl a lift and saved her a bus fare.' Sudden humour entered his voice, and he added, 'Tut, tut, Roxanne. I'm surprised at you!'

Oddly, she thought she would have more easily forgiven him if he had boldly admitted the whole thing. Her tone waspish, she said, 'Only, you see, Delia has been telling *everyone* all about it. She spent the weekend at your flat——'

'She did not!'

'Well, she seems to have a pretty full description of it at her fingertips. Black leather couches, I believe. She's been very full of it all.'

'Did she actually *say* she'd spent the weekend with me?' he demanded.

Momentarily brought up short, Roxanne said, 'I—I don't know. But she certainly hasn't preserved a discreet silence about it. Our Delia isn't burdened with mock modesty, you know. Someone should have warned you that she can't keep a secret——'

Her voice faltered, because Sebastian was laughing, a deep, full-throated laugh of pure enjoyment, and sudden doubt was invading her anger with him.

'Good Lord!' he said, still grinning. 'Someone should certainly have warned me about Delia. I've never met a girl quite like her! And if *you* know her so well, you should have guessed, surely. I met her in town on Thursday, and she mentioned she was going to Auckland to see an aunt at the weekend. I was planning to leave Friday night, and offered her a lift. I picked her up in broad daylight in full view of anyone who happened to be in the main street at the time, and I may be unused to small towns, but I'm not so stupid I'd expect to keep that a secret, exactly! Her aunt lives in South Auckland, my flat is in Parnell, and I had some papers there I wanted to deliver to a guy in Epsom. I stopped off at the flat to collect them, to save me coming all the way back into town after dropping off Delia at her aunt's. It was only polite to ask her in for a drink while I found the papers. She was there about ten minutes, then we left. If she so much as batted an eyelash at me, I'm afraid I was too busy to notice.'

'She said you told her she had very nice legs.'

'I might have, in the car.' He sounded slightly exasperated. 'The girl fishes for compliments all the time. She must have a massive inferiority complex.'

Roxanne blinked. She hadn't thought of that. Delia wasn't interested in compliments from other girls, but she could imagine her pulling up her skirt a little, surveying her legs and saying plaintively, with a sidelong glance, 'I wish I had legs like so-and-so's.' And what could a man say to that, except, 'Your legs are very nice.' Suddenly Delia was less funny than pathetic.

'I see,' she said.

And Sebastian said, 'You'd better. And for having such a nasty mind, you can come out to the house tomorrow and give me a hand in the kitchen. Your mother tells me you're quite useful, given the chance. I've invited a few people for drinks and a swim to return some of the hospitality I've enjoyed since I came.'

He tipped her chin with his hand, kissed her hard and said, 'I'll pick you up after lunch.'

It wasn't until quite a long time later that Roxanne thought he could have asked if she was free, and tried to stir some resentment that he hadn't. But resentment was difficult when her chief emotion was one of almost lightheaded relief that he hadn't been with Delia over the weekend, at all.

CHAPTER FOUR

WHEN Roxanne returned to the house, her father was hovering in the doorway of the lounge.

'Everything all right?' he asked, his eyes anxious.

'Yes,' she said. Hesitating briefly, she added, 'He gave Delia a lift to Auckland, that was all.'

His relief was almost painful to see. 'Of course!' he said, too heartily. 'No man in his right mind would prefer Delia to you.'

Roxanne laughed and, going over to her father, put her arm in his and quickly kissed his cheek. 'You're biased,' she accused affectionately. Then, more soberly, she asked, 'How are things, now, Dad?'

He gave her shoulders a quick squeeze and answered vaguely, 'You're not to worry, my dear. But I'm glad you haven't fallen out with Sebastian.'

'How bad?' she insisted quietly.

He looked at her as though debating within himself, and then confessed, 'About as bad as can be. I don't know how much longer we can hold our heads above water. I'll have to know pretty soon what Sebastian intends to do. And meantime . . .'

'Meantime, we'd better keep on the right side of him,' she finished for him.

He sighed. 'It would certainly help. I wish I could pin him down to a decision, but I don't want to press him. If he knew how weak my position is, in relation to his, it would give him a tremendous advantage, especially if he turns down the merger in the end.'

'You mean, he could use the knowledge against you? Would he do that?'

Owen smiled wryly. 'My dear, he's first and foremost one of the most astute businessmen in the country——'

'Is he? He told me he got his job because it's a family firm.'

'No doubt that had a lot to do with it. But make no mistake, he wouldn't have been put in charge if he didn't have the ability to do the job, and do it well. You only have to look at the profits of Renner Electronics over the last few years to see that he knows exactly what he's doing. To you he may be just a pleasant young man, but he has a reputation for hard-headed dealings in business.'

'A pleasant young man' was hardly how she would have described Sebastian Blair in any circumstances. He had far too positive and forceful a personality for such a lukewarm description. But she let that pass. She murmured, 'Yes, I could imagine he might be ruthless in some ways.'

Rhonda came into the hall, and said, 'Hello—what are you two whispering about?'

'We're not whispering,' Roxanne said calmly. 'Isn't it time you were in bed?'

Rhonda cast her an indignant look, and Roxanne grinned and said, 'Sorry. I keep forgetting you're all grown up and left school. With your hair in two bunches like that, you look about twelve.'

Rhonda grimaced forlornly. 'I tie it up when I put on the freckle lotion, to keep it from getting all gooey.'

'Personally,' their father said, 'I think Doris Day is one of the best-looking women I've seen.'

Rhonda said nothing, but at the look on her face he and Roxanne both started to laugh. 'I see I've put my foot in it again!' Owen grinned, and disappeared in search of his wife.

'*Doris Day*, for heaven's sake!' Rhonda said in disgust, looking after him.

'She's very attractive,' Roxanne pointed out soothingly. Encountering her sister's withering glance, she added solemnly, 'Better than King Kong, anyway.'

'King Kong?' Rhonda goggled, and then broke into laughter. 'You *fool*, Rox!'

They went off to bed together, and Roxanne was still smiling as she switched off the light, but as darkness descended her mind returned to her father's problems, and the smile quickly faded. Things must be really serious. Maybe she could speak to Sebastian, give him a hint . . . But that might make matters worse, betray to him her father's anxiety, and give him the advantage that her father feared. No, there was nothing for it but to wait and see, and keep on good terms with him. But without getting in too deep, she warned herself, recalling those kisses on the beach in the dark. There must be no repetition of that. Worriedly she chewed on her underlip. It was tricky, keeping a man at arm's length without actively repulsing him altogether. On the other hand, he had accepted her refusal readily enough, and had come back prepared to still be at least on friendly terms . . .

When Sebastian called for her the following day, she said, as he started the car, 'I have to be back by seven-thirty. I'm going out tonight.'

'With Mark?'

'Yes.'

'He didn't waste any time, did he?'

Roxanne knew what he meant, of course. But there was no answer to that, and she didn't try to make any.

After a few moments of silence, Sebastian said, 'I don't want you going out with Mark.'

Angrily, she turned in the seat to look at his lean, hard profile. 'You don't have any right to give me orders!' she snapped.

He slanted a brief, unreadable look at her before returning his attention to the winding road ahead of them. 'It wasn't an order,' he said calmly. 'It was a statement of fact.'

Again she was silenced, unable to think of anything to say. Was he telling her he was jealous? The thought was disturbing, because it implied so much about his feelings for her . . .

She looked at him sideways, trying to read his face, but he was giving nothing more away. Surely he didn't feel that strongly about her . . . did he?

He gave no sign of it that afternoon. When they arrived at his house he took her to the kitchen, and she helped to make sandwiches and prepared dips for the potato chips and snack biscuits he had bought. There were two long French loaves, and she found that he had some garlic bulbs, and made garlic butter to spread on them. He watched her and grinned, and said, 'I hope you'll have plenty of that.'

About to say, 'Why?' Roxanne caught the gleam in his eyes and refused to rise to the bait.

People began turning up around three-thirty, and when they had all arrived, a dozen in the end, they strolled down to the beach and swam for about an hour, returning to the house afterwards for drinks and the savouries and sandwiches. Roxanne knew most of them, and as she helped to hand around the food she noticed a few speculative glances, and guessed they were wondering just how far her relationship with Sebastian had progressed. Max Ansell gave her a consciously wicked look and murmured, 'Where's the fair Delia?'

'I've no idea,' Roxanne retorted. 'Why don't you ask Sebastian?'

'Shall I?' He cocked an eyebrow at her and ambled away to pluck at Sebastian's sleeve, and as she sipped a cool glass of cider, she watched the two of them, but since they were half turned from her, admiring the view as they talked, she couldn't see their expressions.

She wondered if Max had the nerve to really ask Sebastian outright about Delia, or even to throw out hints about their supposed weekend together. And what would Sebastian say if he did?

She saw Max laugh at something that Sebastian said, and decided to join them.

They turned as she came up to them, and she didn't hear what they had been talking about. Smiling brightly, she said, 'Max, can I cadge a ride home with you?'

'I'm taking you home,' Sebastian said.

'There's no need,' she protested. 'Max is going that way——'

'No problem,' said Max.

But Sebastian merely told him quite pleasantly, 'Thanks, but I'm taking Roxanne home.'

Max gave Roxanne a look that said very plainly, *So that's how it is!* and moved away from them to speak to someone else.

Roxanne said, 'There's no need for that, you know. I wish you wouldn't be so——'

'So conscientious?' Sebastian suggested, knowing very well that wasn't what she meant. *Obvious—dictatorial—proprietorial*—any of them might have fitted. But he was saying, 'I brought you here, I'm responsible for you. I'll take you home myself.'

'It's quite unnecessary,' she said crossly. 'You can't leave your guests——'

'They're beginning to leave now,' he said. 'They'll be gone by seven. Don't worry, I'll get you back in plenty of time for your date with Mark.' He slipped his arm about her waist, and, hampered by the half full glass in her hand, Roxanne couldn't do a thing to stop him. They were receiving several interested glances, and she looked up at him and hissed, 'Stop it!'

A flicker of annoyance crossed his face, and his fingers on her waist tightened, but then he dropped his arm and walked away from her, joining a group on the opposite side of the room.

When the others had all gone, she was emptying ashtrays and collecting glasses to wash, as he came back into the room after seeing the last couple off.

'Leave that, and come down to the beach for five minutes before we go,' he suggested.

Remembering the last time they had been alone on the beach, she said, 'No, I can't leave it like this. It won't take long.'

He came over and took the ashtray she was holding out of her hand and put it on the nearest table. 'I said, leave it. I can do this when I get back.'

'Well, I'd better get home,' she said stubbornly.

Sebastian looked at his watch. 'There's plenty of time. What's the panic?'

'It's not panic. I just don't want to be late.'

She saw his hand lifting, coming out to catch hers, and she turned away from him and went to stand at the open glass door to the terrace.

'Did Max ask you about Delia?' she asked him.

'Her name was mentioned. Why?'

She shrugged. 'He said he was going to, that's all. I wasn't sure if he was just teasing.'

'Teasing *you* with Delia's name? Did he think you'd be jealous?'

'I don't know. Possibly. You've been doing your best to—stake a claim to me, today, haven't you?'

'I'm glad you noticed. But if it laid you open to Max's teasing, I'm sorry.'

He came to stand close to her, but she wasn't looking at him, her eyes on the breeze-bent manuka and the delicate fronds of ponga growing down the slope to the beach.

Sebastian said, 'I didn't tell Max a thing about Delia. Do you want me to?'

She shook her head. 'It's nothing to do with me.'

'Yes, it is. Don't you want to know *why* I've been "staking a claim", Roxanne?'

She looked at him, then, her eyes deliberately cool. 'You don't like competition, do you?'

'Is that what you think?'

Yes, it was. She said, 'You haven't taken long to learn about small town life, have you? You hoped it would get back to Mark, that I've been acting hostess for you today, that we seem to be on "intimate terms".'

'That's only a part of it. Tell me something—are you on "intimate terms" with Mark?'

'No more than with you,' she said swiftly.

Something flared in his eyes for a second. Then he said, 'It was Mark you were with that first night I met you, wasn't it? It was Mark who'd just been making love to you.'

Roxanne's eyes widened and she felt the heat of a flush on her cheeks. She turned away from him, and his hands came out and jerked her round to face him. 'Did you kiss him the way you kissed me down on the beach?' he demanded.

'Let me go!' she protested. 'That's none of your business.'

'I want—to make it my business,' he said thickly, and pulled her fully into his arms, finding her mouth with a hard, seeking kiss of passion. After a few moments she ceased feeling surprise and bewilderment, conscious only of the muscled warmth of his arms and his body, and the inescapable demands of his mouth on hers. She made a feeble effort at freeing herself, but he wouldn't allow it, perhaps hadn't even noticed. It came to her, with a certain knowledge, that he wasn't going to be satisfied until she responded. Almost unwillingly, she tentatively opened her lips to his invasion, and he took a devastating toll of them, before he released her and held her head in his hands, smoothing back her hair at the temples with his thumbs, his eyes burning on the fullness of her bruised mouth.

'I want you to marry me, Roxanne,' he said huskily. 'Will you?'

She swallowed, her darkened eyes on his face, and his gaze shifted from her mouth and met hers as he repeated, 'Will you?'

I can't, she thought dazedly. She wasn't ready for this, it was totally unexpected.

'I—I don't know,' she said. Her father's anxieties suddenly rose into her mind, and she realised that this could be a crisis point. She couldn't think, though, because his mouth was on hers again, gently seductive, brushing over her lips as he murmured, 'Will this help you make up your mind?'

But when he crushed her mouth again under his, she pushed away strongly, and after a moment he let her go.

'Don't!' she gasped.

'Why not? You've never objected to my kissing you before—except the first time, perhaps.'

'You've never proposed before!' she blurted out.

Sebastian laughed. 'That's true enough. Not to any woman, as a matter of fact.'

'I'm flattered.'

'But not enthusiastic,' he said wryly.

Warnings flashed in her brain like neon signs. She couldn't turn him down, because that would make the merger just about impossible, and it might even make him furious. He could wreck her father's business so easily, and her family's lives in the process.

'I—just wasn't expecting it,' she said feebly. 'Can't I have some time to think about it?'

'While you play me off against Mark?' he asked. 'No, I don't think so.'

'I *wouldn't*! You've no right to say that!'

'Is it Mark you really want?'

'No!'

'Don't look so furious. It did occur to me that you might have been trying to make him jealous of me.'

'Well, I wasn't!'

'No?' He scrutinised her thoroughly, and then his face seemed to relax a trifle. 'All right. I don't understand why you're so surprised now, though. I thought I'd made it plain from the start that I was attracted to you. You've accepted my invitations, and my kisses. I can't say you were exactly forthcoming, barring that time on the beach of course. But you don't appear to find me repulsive.'

'There's a difference between not finding someone repulsive, and wanting to marry them.'

'I see,' he said coldly. 'You've just been playing, have you?'

'No, I haven't! I thought that *you* probably were, though. It never occurred to me that you could be—serious.'

'Why not?'

Roxanne floundered. 'Well, because—you've got money, a good position, you must have plenty of opportunities——'

He smiled. 'I've had some, but I didn't take advantage of them. Have you been seeing me as the Playboy of the Western World?'

She shook her head. 'Of course not. But I hadn't thought of marriage . . .'

'Well, think of it now. How long do you need?'

She opened her mouth to say, *weeks, months.* But then he would probably await her decision before deciding for or against the merger. And her father couldn't afford that sort of delay. With dismay she realised there was only one answer she could give him, to avert catastrophe. With vague thoughts flitting through her mind about breaking the engagement later, once the merger was settled, she said fatalistically, 'I think I've had enough time. The answer is yes.'

For a moment Sebastian didn't move. Then he came close and tipped her chin in his hand and kissed her mouth with enjoyment, but without demand. 'Thank you,' he said. 'Now, I suppose I'd better take you home.'

She heard the question in his voice, and said, 'Yes, please.'

His thumb traced softly over her lips, and he said. 'Still going out with Mark tonight?'

'I've promised,' she reminded him.

'It'll be the last time, then.'

Well, he had the right to demand that now. She swallowed a brief flare of anger, and said, 'Yes.'

'Come on, then.' He dropped his hand and turned away to open the door for her.

In the car, he said, 'Do we tell your family when we get there?'

'No,' said Roxanne. 'Please. It's getting late, and Mark——'

'—might interrupt the celebrations,' he finished. 'Yes, it could be a bit awkward, I guess. When will you tell him?'

'Tonight, I suppose,' she said. 'Can you come over tomorrow and—see the family?'

It would have to happen some time. It might as well be tomorrow.

'Okay,' he said. 'What time?'

'Come for lunch. Mum will like that.'

'She's a marvellous cook, isn't she? I hope her daughter takes after her.'

She couldn't answer his sideways smile. Her throat was locked in sudden fear, at the picture his words conjured up of a cosy domestic future.

When he drew up outside her home, he said, 'I won't come in.' His arm slid along the seat, and she turned her face to his as he bent to kiss her. Her lips felt cold, and the warmth of his almost shocked her. Her response was clumsy and half-hearted, but he smiled at her when he drew back, and said, 'Goodnight, darling. See you tomorrow.'

It was the first time he had called her that, and something strange happened inside her, a sudden plunging of her heart that left her breathless for an instant. 'Goodnight,' she said, getting out of the car quickly, and hurrying into the house without a backward glance.

Afterwards she wondered with a strange sense of guilt if Sebastian had been waiting for her to turn and wave to him. At the time, all she could think about was getting safely into the house and closing the door, as though his presence was a menace she had to get away from.

Mark had booked seats for a film, and although it was one she had wanted to see, she sat through it scarcely taking in the words and actions because she was worrying all the time about how she was going to tell him she was engaged to Sebastian Blair, and whether she should break the news in the morning to her family, or wait for Sebastian to come.

She had supper with Mark afterwards, but it wasn't until they were on their way home in his car that she said, 'I can't go out with you any more, Mark. I'm engaged to Sebastian.'

It sounded bald and very nearly cruel. But she could think of no way of wrapping it up, although she could not quite bring herself to say, 'I'm going to marry Sebastian.'

Mark drove on carefully for some minutes, and then he said, 'Congratulations. He's quite a catch.'

'You know it isn't that,' she said.

'Sorry,' he said after a moment. 'I guess that was sour grapes. Don't you mind about Delia? Or did he do that on purpose to bring you into line?'

'That's a stupid suggestion,' she said. 'Anyway, that actually never happened. He just gave her a lift, that's all.'

Mark laughed. 'Is that what he told you?'

'That's what he told me, and it's true,' she said.

He shrugged elaborately. 'Oh, sure!'

Exasperated, Roxanne gritted her teeth. No one was ever going to believe Sebastian's version of that story, obviously. She supposed the truth was much tamer than the scandal, and therefore less eagerly accepted.

When he stopped at her door, Mark said, 'Do I get a kiss, for old times' sake?'

His voice wobbled a bit at the end, and she said softly, 'Of course. I'm sorry, Mark.'

'So am I!' he said, and kissed her long and fiercely.

He drew back breathing hard, and she slipped out of the car feeling troubled and pitying. She had always enjoyed Mark's kisses before, until he went too far. This time she had felt nothing but sadness for him, and a longing to get it over and done with. She wouldn't have married him anyway, she was certain of that, now. But Sebastian had hurried their parting, and she faintly resented that.

Before Sebastian came the next day, Roxanne had had most of the morning to keep asking herself what on earth she had done, and wonder how she was going to get out of it. But always she came to the inescapable conclusion that she could have done nothing else. Of course she couldn't marry Sebastian to save her father's business—the idea was preposterous—but presented with the dilemma that he had put her in, how could she risk the consequences of a refusal?

She thought of going to her father and telling him what had happened, asking for his advice. But she had a very good idea what he would do. He wouldn't countenance a 'marriage of convenience' for a moment, and the idea of her remaining engaged to Sebastian until the merger was finalised would horrify him almost as much, perhaps more. He would probably take it on himself to tell Sebastian she wasn't going to marry him, after all. And she guessed that Sebastian would find that even more humiliating than if she had refused him herself. And humiliation might make him vindictive.

She would have to see him herself, before he had a chance to announce their 'engagement' to the family. She would tell him she had made a mistake—been carried away by his lovemaking, or dazzled by his money—anything.

But again there was the concrete wall of the fact that her father could not afford to lose the opportunity of the merger. And what man would want to enter into a close business relationship with the father of the girl who had refused his offer of marriage?

And how would he feel about being bound into a partnership with the father of a girl who had jilted him before they reached the altar? a small, grim voice within her enquired.

By then it would be too late to undo the merger, and surely she could find some way of breaking off the engagement by mutual consent, eventually. Or at least of persuading him to release her without too many hard feelings. Engagements were broken every day, after all; people did make mistakes. And if things became—awkward—afterwards, she could go back to Auckland until the whole thing had blown over.

Answering the small, insistent voice of conscience, she told herself that surely Sebastian wouldn't be too hurt. He didn't seem desperately in love with her, and in fact she had been genuinely surprised by his proposal. Of course, he liked making love to her, she had never doubted that he found her desirable and liked her company. But that, she thought dispassionately, was probably about all it amounted to. He had begun a new phase of his life, buying a house here, he was of an age to marry and settle with a family, and no doubt she could be regarded as a suitable wife. Which might mean that he was seriously considering the merger, too. He had made love to her with insistent passion only once, and when she put a stop to it he had accepted it with good grace. Surely he wasn't carried away by his feelings for her? In a few months' time, whatever he did feel for her might have burnt itself out.

Rationalising, the inner voice jeered, but no matter which way she looked at it, the crux of the problem remained. At least this would give her father a chance, and couldn't the future be allowed to take care of itself, once the pressing matter of the merger was solved?

Some time during the morning the decision made itself, and Roxanne found herself wondering instead whether she should give her father a hint before Sebastian arrived. Because he might suspect her motives in accepting Sebastian, and he mustn't be allowed to do that.

Dismayed, she realised that she was going to have to pretend, to her father, and to everyone, that she was a pleased and happy bride-to-be. In the event, it didn't prove as difficult as she expected. She had a quiet word with her father, and although he was surprised, she realised that sheer relief made him eager to accept that she was genuinely in love with Sebastian, and that nothing could be more natural. That hurdle over, it was relatively easy to accept Sebastian's possessive kiss on his arrival, and to tell him quietly that, although she had told her father their news, no one else had been informed.

'Mark?' he asked, his eyes keen on her face, and she nodded and turned away.

He took her wrist and made her look at him again. 'How did he take it?'

'Quite well,' she said coolly. 'And that's all I'm going to tell you, Sebastian. He has nothing to do with—with us, now.'

His brows rose a fraction, but he said, 'Fair enough. When do we tell your mother and Rhonda?

She shrugged. 'Whenever you like.'

'Before lunch?'

'All right.' With an effort at lightheartedness she said, 'I wouldn't be surprised if Dad produces a bottle of something to celebrate with.'

He did—not champagne but a very good New Zealand sparkling wine from the Te Kauwhata district, and although the celebration and the excited banter over lunch seemed unreal to Roxanne, she did notice that Sebastian appeared more relaxed and happy than she had ever seen him before. He smiled often, and laughed outright once or twice when Rhonda teased him, and his eyes when they rested on Roxanne held a warmth which made her glance away from him in confused panic. For the first time it occurred to her that the hardest part of this charade might be ensuring that Sebastian didn't guess at her motives. As her fiancé, he might well expect certain privileges that she was scarcely prepared to allow him.

After lunch, the girls helped their mother with the dishes, and Owen took Sebastian off to his study. 'Is he going to ask Sebastian about his prospects?' Rhonda asked, laughing. But Roxanne, aiming a half-hearted swipe at her sister with a tea-towel, speculated on whether they were discussing the merger. She didn't think her father would be clumsy enough to bring it up so soon, but she hoped that Sebastian might.

Later, the family left her alone with him out by the pool, in the shade of one of the jacarandas her mother had planted years ago. As they watched Rhonda being led rather reluctantly away by her mother, Sebastian grinned down at Roxanne and said, 'Well, shall we take advantage of their tact?'

She turned away, smiling but embarrassed, and shook her head slightly. Sebastian caught her hand, keeping her by him, and said, 'Would you disappoint them?'

'They won't know.'

'I will.'

She looked up at him, and he was smiling, his eyes teasing as he noted the faint flush on her cheeks. He looked very attractive, and for a moment the fantastic thought entered her head that really it would be no hardship to marry him.

He quirked an eyebrow at her, and tugged gently at her hand to bring her nearer. The realisation that she was hardly acting like a newly engaged girl hit her with a sudden chill, and she raised her lips to his and let him kiss her.

The touch of his mouth was light and almost tantalising, moving softly over hers, but the kiss lasted only seconds. Sebastian raised his head and ran a forefinger down her cheek, pushed a strand of hair behind her ear, and gently stroked the lobe, then closed his hand lightly on her throat. 'I think you're inhibited by your family,' he told her. 'Wait until I get you alone out at my place.'

Fear made her tense, suddenly. She stirred, and his hands dropped from her. 'Is that a threat?' she asked, trying to match his teasing.

'Scared?' he jeered softly, laughing.

'Maybe.' She had moved away from him, her hands lightly touching the fragile-looking flowers that starred an oleander, as she went from the shade into the sun.

His hands descended on her shoulders from behind, and turned her firmly to face him.

'Don't be,' he said. And now his expression was quite serious and almost intense. 'There's no need, I promise you.'

It steadied her, but she couldn't meet his eyes. Almost childishly, she dropped her head against his shoulder, and felt his lips graze her temple before she raised her head again and pushed away from him.

He let her walk a little way, then hooked an arm about her waist as they strolled together back to the house.

It wasn't until much later that it occurred to her that the reassurance had been for the girl Sebastian thought had promised to marry him, not for one who was planning to cheat him. She had the distinct feeling that he would be much less understanding if he ever found out just why she had agreed to an engagement.

CHAPTER FIVE

The official announcement of the engagement went into the local paper the following Saturday, and after a day of answering congratulatory telephone calls, Roxanne and her family were glad to accept Sebastian's suggestion that they should all spend the next day at his house. He had no telephone as yet, though it had been promised, and the prospect of a day of peace was a blessing.

It was Rhonda who asked, over a cold picnic lunch which Bettina had insisted on packing for them all, when Sebastian and Roxanne would be getting married.

Sebastian said promptly, 'Soon.' And Roxanne said, 'We haven't decided yet.'

Later in the afternoon, the two of them went for a walk along the beach, while Owen and Bettina dozed quietly on the terrace, and Rhonda sat absorbed in sketching the paper-winged pink berries of an akeake.

Out of sight of the house, Sebastian asked her, 'How soon will you marry me, Roxanne?'

Her eyes on the restless uncurling of the sea as it touched the shore, she hesitated. How long would it take to make the merger watertight? she wondered uneasily. She couldn't ask him *that*.

'I've hardly got used to the idea of being engaged yet,' she said evasively. 'I haven't really thought about it.'

Sebastian stopped walking and caught her hands in his, smiling down at her. 'Well, give it some thought,' he said, and bent his head to kiss her cheek and slide his lips down her throat till they rested in the curve of her shoulder. She was wearing shorts and a cool cotton top held by narrow straps over her shoulders. His thumb hooked under one strap and slipped it down her arm, as his lips wandered across her bared skin. He, too, wore shorts, and had discarded his shirt, revealing a tanned chest with a sprinkling of crisp dark curling hair. His other hand slid under her loose top on to the smooth skin of her back, his fingers caressing her spine as he pulled her closer.

Desire kindled insidiously inside her, as the hand that had moved her strap came back softly over her shoulder and down to caress the exposed upper curve of her breast.

Stirring restlessly in his arms, Roxanne complained huskily, 'I can't think at all when you do that!'

He laughed softly and both arms went about her to haul her closer to him as he found her mouth with his and kissed her with deep, lazy enjoyment. Her hands flattened against his chest, and she felt the wiriness of the black hair curling between her fingers, and the steady thud of his heart against her palm. His thighs were warm and hard-muscled, and one of them parted hers slightly, pushing against her in blood-rushing intimacy.

After a few moments she knew that she was kissing him back, her lips parting willingly to his exploration, and her body unashamedly moulding itself into the contours of his. Her hands went up to his shoulders, and she was still clinging blindly when he took away his mouth and muttered, 'Marry me soon, Roxanne. I want to make love to you for ever.'

Disorientated, she stared at him almost blankly, while the dizzy world righted itself and moved back into focus. Then, suddenly appalled at the depth of the response that he had wrung from her, she pulled herself away.

'Oh, don't!' she said confusedly, her hands going up

to her flaming cheeks.

Sebastian laughed again, and looked at her curiously. 'Don't make love to you?' he asked. 'Why not?'

It was a legitimate question, she realised. She was supposed to be going to marry him, after all. And here she was going all to pieces over a mere kiss.

Even while she tried to pull herself together and frame words for an acceptable plausible answer, Sebastian said slowly, 'I do believe I've got myself an old-fashioned country girl.' He paused. 'Have I?'

Well, he had, at that, if he meant what she thought he did. Stalling for time while she collected her wits, she said, 'You make me sound like Bo-Peep!'

He laughed at that, briefly and low. 'Hardly. I didn't mean you were—unsophisticated. But I suspect that you're an innocent, all the same.'

Well, it couldn't do any harm to admit that, she supposed. In fact, there might be definite advantages. 'Oh, we're a very old-fashioned family,' she said, 'My mother is looking forward to planning a white wedding with all the trimmings. It'll take ages to make the arrangements.'

'Will it?' He was looking at her rather penetratingly, his face thoughtful. 'What does that mean? Weeks? Months?'

'Months, I expect,' Roxanne said quickly, trying to sound regretful. 'But we can't deprive her of it, you know. She's only got two daughters, and—and she'll want to launch us in style.'

'Now, *that* sounds like a battleship, not a bride,' he commented, and she giggled with relief. But then he added, 'I'm not a very patient man. It had better not be too long.'

Rather tartly, she said, 'Don't I have any say in the matter?'

'Yes, of course. But you seem rather reluctant to make a definite decision. What's the matter, Roxanne?

Getting cold feet?'

'Well, I—I don't think we should rush into anything,' she said vaguely. 'We haven't really known each other very long, have we?'

'Long enough, I thought,' he said, a rather wry smile on his lips. 'Will two months give you enough time to get used to the idea of marrying me?'

Two months. Was it long enough? Roxanne didn't know. Somehow she would have to find out how long she had before the merger was finalised. 'Let me talk to my parents,' she said. 'Please—before we set a firm date.'

He looked a little cool, but he inclined his head and said, 'All right. We'll postpone the decision for now.'

Relieved, she turned to walk back the way they had come, and Sebastian took her hand to stroll beside her.

'You're very close to your parents, aren't you?' he asked.

'Yes, we're a close family. Isn't yours?'

'No, not really, I guess. My father died a few years ago, and I suppose in the months before that I was closer to him than I had ever been as a child. He knew the end was coming, and he was anxious to leave the business flourishing.'

'For his family's sake?'

'I'm not sure. I think the business had become an end in itself, by that time. My mother was never particularly interested in it, and my only sister married an Australian and went to live over the Tasman.'

'You said it was your mother who was a Renner.'

'That's right. My father married the boss's daughter, and gained control of the company.'

'But that wasn't the reason, surely . . .?' she protested, rather shocked by the cynical expression on his face.

Sebastian shrugged. 'How would I know? But it was hardly the love-match of the century. By the time I grew up they'd virtually ceased to communicate, although they still lived in the same house.'

'That's awfully sad,' she said. 'How terrible for them! And for you.'

'I suppose it was.' He looked down at her troubled face and said, 'Don't let it bother you—it's all water under the bridge, anyway, and I grew up relatively unscathed, I believe. I wasn't exactly a deprived child.'

She slanted him a smile, but her expression, as they moved out of the sun into the shade of a grove of tall karakas, was preoccupied. Their feet scuffed at the dry sand, and woolly hare-tail grass brushed their ankles as they trod on to the low hillocks at the edge of the beach. Sebastian suddenly said, 'Roxanne, has your father mentioned a possible merger between Renners and his firm?'

Her heart seemed to stop in fright. She tripped over an exposed root of marram grass, and he steadied her with a hard hand on her waist.

'Well, has he?' he persisted, when she had regained her balance.

'Why?' she choked out.

'Because I just wondered if perhaps you had some crazy idea that I asked you to marry me in order to—facilitate a merger. You haven't, have you?'

Relief and guilt flooded through her in equal parts. Slightly hysterically, she laughed. 'Of course not!' she assured him. 'The thought never entered my head.'

That was the truth, but now a horrible fear assailed her that he might guess her real reason for accepting him. She had to make sure he didn't. Almost feverishly, she threw her arms about his neck and for the first time offered him the invitation of her lips, whispering, 'Where would I get such an idiotic idea?'

'Not from me,' he said huskily, and his mouth crushed hers hungrily, in a long, merciless, draining kiss.

Roxanne responded ardently, at first with calculation, to make him forget their dangerous conversation, and then because the sweetness of passion took over, and she simply couldn't help herself. When he thrust her away almost violently, she looked at him in bewilderment, stunned both by the force of her own response and the suddenness of his action.

'Sorry, darling,' he said, putting a warm arm about her shoulders, and turning her firmly to walk on. 'I want to lay you down right here on the sand and make love to you properly, but you wouldn't like that, would you? You want your white wedding first.'

She didn't answer, too shaken by the realisation that if he had pulled her down with him on to the sand and the rough grasses she might have found it very hard to deny him what he wanted.

Don't get carried away, she warned herself. Sex, that was all it was, a purely biological response to an attractive man who seemed rather expert at arousing such responses. And proximity, she supposed, had a lot to do with it. After all, she had responded fairly passionately to Mark on occasion. Sebastian wasn't the only man who could strike chords of passion in her. The fact that he seemed able to find them and play on them more readily and more effectively than anyone else ever had could be due to her own growing maturity, or his skill, or simply the odd circumstances that had compelled her to accept his caresses in the first place. Heavens, she didn't even *like* him; from the first he had produced prickles of antagonism. Thank heaven he seemed willing to accept and respect the principles her upbringing had instilled, anyway. It would make the part she had to play a great deal easier.

She dared not mention the merger again to Sebastian, but by apparently casual questions put to her father she managed to discover that the deal was definitely on and that it might take two months to complete the arrangements. Knowing she could scarcely jilt Sebastian the minute the papers were signed, she suggested a spring wedding, near the end of the year.

She sensed Sebastian's exasperation immediately, but his voice was even as he said, 'That's just about nine months away.'

They were in his car, on their way to visit friends of his in Auckland. The road wound down over the hills towards the wide sweep of Orewa beach, where the waves below spread like lace-edged silk along the smooth shore. He pulled into a parking bay overlooking the beach and turned with his arm on the steering wheel to look at her.

'I know,' she said. 'But it's Autumn already, and winter weddings are too cold.'

'*You* won't be cold, I promise you,' he interjected.

Her pulses quickened alarmingly, but she said, 'Seriously——'

'Yes—*seriously*,' he said grimly.

'I want a nice wedding,' she said stubbornly. 'Pretty dresses and sunshine and flowers. It only happens once in a lifetime, after all . . .' It all sounded petty and silly, and she cast about desperately for some reason that would convince him. 'I want to look beautiful for you,' she said finally, her eyes consciously pleading.

His face was closed, his dark eyes disconcertingly keen on her face, but his expression softened slightly at that, and he said, 'You'd look beautiful in sackcloth—you can't help it. Is all this really so important to you, or are you just pleasing your family?'

Of course it wasn't important; if she loved him she would have married him in sackcloth in the middle of a snowstorm, if she had to. About to say, yes, it was something she'd dreamed about all her life, she found the lie sticking in her throat. Before she could answer him he had taken her chin firmly in his hand, so that she couldn't turn away, and was saying quietly, 'You know, I could have sworn that you're not the type to want your wedding to be a sort of sideshow. I know you're very fond of your mother, and no doubt she does want to do the thing properly and see you sail down the aisle in your long white gown, with a retinue of bridesmaids, and have all the uncles and aunts and remote cousins drinking your health later at a slap-up wedding breakfast. But what do *you* really want?'

His eyes were still on her face, and they demanded an answer. She sensed danger, thought she saw a dawning of hard suspicion in his gaze, and said hastily, 'Of course I'd like a nice wedding, something to look back on later, and I don't want to disappoint my mother. But it isn't really important, Sebastian. If you want a quiet wedding, I won't mind at all.'

He let her go, and said rather irritably, 'It isn't that—you've missed the point. I don't care how many friends and relations your people want to invite, or how many bridesmaids you want. You can have it as elaborate as you like—but soon! Not next spring!'

Roxanne looked away from him, biting her lip, and he said roughly, 'Sometimes I wonder if you really want to marry me at all.'

Alarm showed in her face as she twisted to face him. 'Of course I do!' she cried. Her hand went out to his where it rested on the wheel, and he caught her fingers and raised them to his mouth, moving his lips against her palm.

'I'm sorry, darling,' he said. 'I suppose I'm frustrated, and bad-tempered with it. Tell me I don't have to wait nine months for you?'

Her heart hammering, she said, 'Well, would—three months do? That would make it in May.'

'All right,' he said, after a moment. 'May. That should give your mother ample time to organise it.'

Sebastian told his friends, almost as soon as the introductions were made and their congratulations accepted, that the wedding date was in May. Neal Osborne clapped him on the shoulder, winked at Roxanne and said, 'Good for you, mate.' And his wife, Felicia, gave her an odd look and flashed a smile at Sebastian that made Roxanne strangely uneasy.

They were a striking couple, Neal as tall as Sebastian, but more thickset and with wavy fair hair. His blue eyes were friendly, with a glint of masculine appreciation in them as he smiled at Roxanne. His wife was quite different, a small, exquisitely made woman with extremely slender ankles and wrists giving her an air of fragility, although her figure bordered on the voluptuous. Her hair was as dark as Sebastian's, worn long and straight, well brushed and gleaming subtly where it caught the light. She wore small gold hoops in her ears that gave her an exotic look, and her eyes were the only truly violet eyes that Roxanne had ever seen, an incredible shade of deep purplish-blue. She had clear, faintly gold skin and was wearing a clinging dark blue dress that had a side slit to the top of her thigh. Roxanne, in a full-skirted dress with a wide neckline and tiny sleeves, of soft cream cotton, felt suddenly dowdy and far too tall.

The Osbornes had no children, and Roxanne gathered from the conversation in their large, beautifully furnished lounge that they had been married for over ten years. Surprised, she glanced at Felicia. She must be nearing thirty, at least, but the years seemed to have been held at bay. No one would have guessed her age at anything over twenty-five, and except for her air of sophistication, she could have passed for eighteen or twenty at first sight.

Sebastian had told her that he and Neal had been at university together, and been friends ever since. Neal had a law degree, and handled Renner's legal affairs. But the talk today was not of business. This was entirely a social occasion. The afternoon was spent talking and listening to records played on an elaborate stereo set-up which was Neal's pride and joy.

On the way home, Sebastian asked, 'Did you enjoy yourself?'

'Yes,' Roxanne replied cautiously. 'You've known them a long time, haven't you?'

'Yes, I suppose I have.'

'Both of them?'

'I was best man at Neal's wedding,' he said. 'Before that I'd never laid eyes on Felicia.'

'I'll bet it was a shock,' she commented.

His eyes sharp, he said, 'What do you mean?'

'Well, she's a stunner.'

'So she is,' he agreed carelessly. And then, with an odd inflection, he added, 'She's not popular with women, I believe. Did you like her?'

'That's an unfair question. I don't dislike her. But it's difficult to say whether you like a person or not on a few hours' acquaintance. I don't think she would be an easy person to get close to.'

'Perhaps not,' he said, and changed the subject.

Roxanne had not met his mother, who preferred to live in Wellington, but Mrs Blair had sent a correct, one-page letter to Roxanne expressing a distant pleasure in the engagement, and looking forward to meeting her. At the wedding, Roxanne supposed. Well, there wasn't going to be one, so that was one pleasure they would both have to forgo.

Without arousing suspicion, it had been difficult to restrain her family, and especially her mother, from carrying out expensive and irrevocable preparations for the supposed marriage date. She staved off as much as she could, with repeated assurances that there was plenty of time, and she firmly vetoed an engagement party, on the grounds that the wedding was so close it was pointless, anyway. Her mother disagreed, but reluctantly dropped the idea.

Roxanne and Sebastian did attend parties, though, and had to run a gauntlet of congratulations and teasing which embarrassed Roxanne but which Sebastian fielded with ease.

Max Ansell pressed them to attend a party to celebrate some real estate coup, and it wasn't until they had been in his crowded lounge for more than ten minutes that Roxanne noticed that Delia was also present. Catching her look, Delia gave her a nervous smile and turned away, pale hair swinging on narrow shoulders that were bared by the gold and white striped strapless sheath that shamelessly hugged her curves. A hand holding a narrow-stemmed glass waved about dangerously as she chattered to Max, smiling and tossing her hair, while the other hand touched pink-tipped nails to his sleeve.

When Max took her by the arm and brought her over to Sebastian and Roxanne, she was still smiling, but it had gone a bit stiff, and Roxanne felt her own facial muscles tightening. She looked at Max and saw that he was enjoying creating a 'situation', and realised that, about them, the chatter of the party was slowly dying as people became aware of what was happening. *Damn you, Max*, she thought, shooting him a furious look, and then she was smiling back at Delia, who was saying much too loudly and brightly, 'Congratulations, you two, on your engagement. I think it's just fantastic, and I'm *sure* you'll be *very* happy. It couldn't have happened to nicer people!'

Her hand came out and fluttered over Sebastian's sleeve, then lightly touched Roxanne's hand, before it went to join the other one that was clutching at her glass.

They murmured polite thanks, then Sebastian said

casually, 'Oh, by the way, about that time I gave you a lift to Auckland——'

Almost under her breath, Delia said, 'Yes?' But the room was so quiet now that everyone must have heard.

Everyone couldn't see the look in her eyes, though, like a cornered rabbit waiting for a death blow. Sebastian paused, and Roxanne spoke quickly, her hand going to his arm, the fingers digging into the sleeve of his jacket until he must feel the urgency of the message she was trying to communicate. 'Darling, that was before you got engaged to *me*. I'm sure Delia understands.' Ignoring the slightly startled look in his eyes, she turned her attention to Delia, and added sweetly, with a touch of humour, 'Sebastian has been perfectly honest with me, Delia, no hard feelings. But from now on I don't let him out of my sight—you *do* understand, don't you? Sebastian isn't available for any more—er—lifts.'

Relief, gratitude, puzzlement, flashed over Delia's face. Someone in the background gave a smothered guffaw, and a couple of giggles were quickly covered by chatter.

Max rocked back a little on his heels, his hands dug into his pockets while he looked thoughtfully from Delia's face to Roxanne's. Sebastian was looking enigmatic, his eyes fixed on Roxanne. He moved his arm experimentally, and Roxanne's grip on it relaxed and fell. He took her empty glass and put out his hand for Delia's that was almost drained too. 'Can I get you another?' he asked her politely. 'What are you drinking?'

'Bacardi and Coke,' she said automatically, and he disappeared through the crowd to the kitchen where the drinks were laid out.

Delia said quickly, and very quietly, to Roxanne, 'He only gave me a ride, you know. He *did* tell you, didn't he?'

'Yes, I know. You went to see your aunt.'

Max said curiously, 'Did you believe him?'

'Yes, I did.' Roxanne looked at Max levelly. 'Have we disappointed you?'

'Oh, no,' he said, grinning broadly. 'I'm hugely entertained.'

Delia looked at him for the first time, and with an odd, quiet dignity she said, 'You bastard, Max!' and, turning on her heel, walked away, her back very straight.

One of the men caught her about the waist, and she struggled briefly, then Roxanne saw her thin shoulders droop as she allowed him to pull her into the circle of his arm and nuzzle at her cheek.

Max was watching, too, his face unusually flushed. He looked back at Roxanne almost angrily and asked, '*Did* she go to see her old aunt?'

'I'm sure of it.'

'Well, why the hell did she spread that story, then——!'

'Max,' Roxanne explained gently, 'Delia has her reputation to consider.'

He gave a harsh crack of laughter. '*Reputation*, for God's sake!' he grated. Then she saw that the anger in his eyes was unmistakable, and he said slowly, turning to watch Delia giggle at something the man who had caught her was whispering into her ear, 'The stupid little bitch!'

Sebastian came back with the girls' drinks, looked about for Delia, and Max said rather grimly, 'She's over there. I'll take it.'

Roxanne caught at his sleeve and said softly, 'You won't give her away, will you?'

'To this lot? No,' he said. 'But I'll damn well give her something to think about!'

'What was that all about?' Sebastian asked, handing Roxanne her glass.

'What?' she asked absently, watching Max as he almost forcibly extricated Delia from the other man's embrace and marched her out of the room, firmly closing the door behind them.

'Well, for starters, that axe job you just did on my attempt to clear my reputation in this town. You did realise that I could have made Delia admit that we didn't go away for a dirty weekend together?'

'Yes' she said. 'That's just what I was afraid of. Do you mind very much?'

'I thought I was doing something for *your* pride,' he said. 'Maybe I should have checked with you first, but I didn't know the opportunity was going to present itself.'

'Oh, it didn't present itself, exactly,' she said dryly. 'Max set it up.'

'So I gathered. Why, do you suppose?'

'I think, mainly because he enjoys manipulating situations like that. But also—I suspect he wanted to give Delia a jolt.'

'Well,' he said, after a moment or two, 'somebody should.'

Roxanne smiled. 'I think he's just had a bit of a jolt himself. How do you suppose a man feels when he discovers he's in love with someone like Delia?'

His gaze suddenly very austere, Sebastian said, 'Why ask me?'

Roxanne shrugged. 'You're a man.'

'I'll tell you how he'd feel,' Sebastian said deliberately. 'He'd feel angry and disgusted, and violent. If you're as concerned for Delia as you seem to be, I think if I were you I'd mount a rescue operation fairly soon.'

Roxanne's eyes widened. 'Are you serious?' She glanced towards the door through which Max had virtually dragged Delia five minutes before. It led into a passageway, with the bathroom and Max's bedroom and spare room opening off it.

'I'm serious,' Sebastian added.

Roxanne looked about at the crowded room, heard the laughter and chat, and the music that was thudding out from a record player in the corner. 'He couldn't——' she said. And Sebastian asked,

'Who'd hear her if she screamed?'

Shocked, she stared wordlessly into his grim face, then put down her drink on a nearby bookcase, and started for the door to the passageway.

Sebastian followed, and closed the door behind them, muffling the noise of the party.

The bathroom door and the door of the spare bedroom were ajar, but the other door was closed, and from behind it came the sound of Max's voice, not raised but with a coldly vicious note, interrupted by Delia's sudden shrill, angry protest. Then something glass smashed, a shocking sound, and Max laughed loudly and harshly, and Delia's voice rose, wobbled and dissolved into loud sobbing.

Sebastian pushed aside Roxanne as she made to open the door, and his knuckles fell hard on the door. 'Are you all right in there?' he demanded.

There was no reply, but even as he touched the handle the door was flung open and Max stood there, his eyes gleaming with anger and his face strangely pale.

Roxanne said, 'We heard Delia crying. Can I help?'

He looked from her to Sebastian, and smiled with understanding cynicism. 'It's all right,' he drawled. 'I haven't attacked her or beaten her – though she's been asking for one or the other for years. Well, some other poor fellow might oblige her, not me. I wouldn't touch the little slut with a barge-pole—I just told her so. That's when she threw the lamp at me, she's a hellcat as well . . .'

'I think that's enough, don't you?' said Sebastian, quite pleasantly.

Max looked at him, and some of the anger died as he looked slightly shamefaced. He shrugged, then slouched out of the doorway, and Sebastian said, 'Shall we go back to the party, and leave the girls alone?'

'Sure,' said Max, and moved aside to let Roxanne into the room. 'Watch out for broken glass,' he said. He put his hand up to a trickle of blood oozing from a tiny cut in his cheek, and pulled out a handkerchief to wipe it. Looking at the red smear, he laughed a little unsteadily, and said 'It's a great party!'

Roxanne shut the door on them and stepped over the broken lamp to sit on the bed, where Delia lay on the rumpled cover, curled into a miserable heap, with her face pressed against the pillow.

Her whole body shuddered with sobs, the ugly, tearing sound of them making Roxanne's throat ache in sympathy. She said helplessly, 'Delia—Delia, he didn't mean it. He'll be sorry later, you know.'

The tumbled blonde head shook vehemently, as Delia gasped out, 'He did! He—meant—every—horrible word. He said—he called me——' Again she shook her head, as though trying to deny the memory of it, and Roxanne put a soothing hand on her hair and began stroking it.

'He was angry,' she said. 'He didn't know what he was saying.'

The sobs were quieting a little. 'Oh yes, he did!' Delia said bitterly, turning a little on the bed, so that Roxanne could see half her face, flushed and tear-stained and with streaks of mascara giving her a woe-begone look. 'I h-hate him!' she cried fiercely, but the tears welled again in her eyes, and she pulled up a corner of the bedspread and buried her face in it.

Roxanne let her cry, putting an arm about the girl's shoulder and rocking her gently for comfort. Eventually Delia scrubbed fiercely at her face with the bedspread, then looked at the marks she had made on it and said with watery satisfaction, 'I've got mascara all over his damned bedspread, and I hope it *never* washes out!'

Roxanne laughed and said, 'And serve him right!'

'Well, he *was* a bastard, doing that to you and Sebastian—and me,' Delia said resentfully. 'It was a rotten trick. I knew he was wild, but when he hauled me in here, I was scared. Well, what do *you* do when a man scares you, Rox? We're not as s-strong as—as they are, and you can only try and sweeten them up a bit and make them forget about being angry, can't you?' She blinked away fresh tears. 'I just put my arms round his neck, and said, "You shouldn't be such a beast, Maxie. Then people wouldn't call you names." I thought we'd kiss and make up, and maybe he'd make a pass, but nothing could *happen*, I mean, in the middle of a party—he doesn't have *that* kind of party, does he? And th-then he—he k-kissed me, but it was *horrible*, because he just wanted to—hurt me. And he *threw* me down on the bed, and I was t-terrified. And then he leaned over me and said wasn't that what I was after, and began—t-telling me what he thought of me, what *everyone* thinks of me, he said. He said the girls all laugh at me, and the men—the men—t-talk about me in the pub, and that I'm the—the "easiest lay in town"! Oh, God, Rox, I feel so—so *dirty*!'

'I'm sure it isn't true,' Roxanne said, trying to instil conviction into her voice. 'He was just trying to hurt you, that's all.'

'Yes,' Delia said tonelessly. And then, her face lifting to Roxanne's with the bewilderment of a child who has been beaten for an unknown misdemeanour, she asked '*Why?*'

Carefully, Roxanne said, 'I think he's just found out that he's fonder of you than he wants to be. And it's made him a bit unreasonable—temporarily.'

'Max?' Delia queried, amazed. 'Fond of *me*?' Her tear-washed blue eyes widened, and then she said, 'No. Oh, heck, no. Not Max. You've got it wrong.'

'Maybe,' Roxanne conceded. 'Delia, Max knows you didn't spend that weekend with Sebastian. But I'm afraid everyone else thinks you did. And it's partly my fault, I know. I thought that—that you——'

'That I wanted everyone to think that,' Delia said, flushing. 'Well, I did. And I think it was just super of you, tonight, to let them go on thinking it. Only—only Max made it seem—different, somehow. I sort of thought it seemed glamorous and—interesting. But he made it sound cheap and sordid. He made *everything* I do sound cheap and sordid.'

'I'm sure it isn't.' Roxanne said gently. 'Maybe sometimes you've been unwise, and sometimes a bit too trusting, and too—loving.'

Delia looked at her strangely, and Roxanne said, 'Surely that isn't such a crime?'

'Thank you,' said Delia, with an access of that odd dignity with which she had walked away from Max in the lounge. 'But you see, I don't think I *have* been very loving. I just wanted to be—admired. I guess I'm not a very nice person, really. I was always so jealous of people like you, at school, and after—you were always so pretty, and so popular, and you had a nice home, and super clothes, and I thought, one day I'll make it. One day they'll all be jealous of *me*. and I *did*—at least, I thought I had, until Max——'

With something like awe, Roxanne remembered the plump and unprepossessing teenager who had blossomed into Delia the Blonde Bombshell and, thinking of the effort and will-power that had achieved that transformation, she said, 'Delia, you set out to do something, and you certainly did it. Believe me, you've created havoc among the menfolk and panic in the women.'

'Max said they laugh at me——' Delia whispered, her head hanging.

'Sarah Hancock wasn't laughing when Derek was making an idiot of himself over you,' Roxanne said firmly. 'And neither was Molly Sampson when *her* boy-friend took one look at you and left her for dead.'

Delia's head came up, and gleam of hope and a sort of naïve pleasure entered her blue eyes. 'No, they weren't, were they?' she said almost eagerly. 'Did *you* mind, when you thought that Sebastian and I——'

'That was before we were engaged,' Roxanne said firmly. Then she said honestly, 'But yes, I did, a bit.'

'Oh. I'm sorry. You've been so nice . . . I never really meant to hurt anyone.'

'The thing is, Delia,' Roxanne said carefully, 'you've certainly got what you thought you wanted, but is it really worth it? Maybe if you set yourself a different goal, you could go after something more——'

'More worthwhile?'

'Well—yes.'

Her tousled head drooping again, Delia whispered, 'I suppose making people jealous and tying men in knots isn't really much of a life's ambition.'

'Well, it's—unusual, anyway,' Roxanne admitted dryly, and Delia gave a faint giggle.

'So where do I go from here?' she said mournfully, a moment later. 'With a reputation like I've got, how can I ever expect people to see me any differently?'

'It won't be easy,' Roxanne admitted. 'But if you want to create a new image for yourself—well, it won't be the first time, will it? And you were jolly successful before.'

Delia grimaced. 'I could give it a try, I suppose. Let my hair go back to its natural colour, and wear different clothes.' She sighed, and picked up a strand of her hair, squinting down at it. 'Pity—I like being a blonde.'

'There's no need to alter it, if you don't want to,' said Roxanne. 'You don't have to change your appearance completely. It's more a matter of behaving differently. People will soon get the message. Well, sooner or later, they will, if you're really determined.'

Delia nodded, and stood up, going over to the large dressing table mirror. 'Lor!' she exclaimed in horror. 'What a fright I look!'

'You'll have to wash your face,' Roxanne smiled, coming to stand beside her. 'And your hair could do with a comb.'

Delia looked at their two reflections in the mirror, herself in the clinging gold and white dress, her curls tumbling round her face, and Roxanne in a slim-fitting skirt and filmy blouse, with her shining hair pulled back in a simple filigree clasp.

'*You're* blonde,' Delia said. 'But you never look like a—a tart.'

'Neither do you. Only some of your clothes are a bit—obvious, I suppose. My mother used to quote me something when I was about fourteen and wearing skin-tight jeans—you remember, we all did! "Clothes," she said, "should be tight enough to show that you're a woman, and loose enough to show that you're a lady".'

Delia laughed. 'I'll remember that,' she promised

'Come along to the bathroom,' Roxanne offered, 'and I'll help you remove the remains of the mascara, and do your hair for you.'

By the time they returned to the party Delia was a little pink-eyed, and she looked a good deal less made up than usual. Roxanne thought it an improvement, although Delia had bewailed the fact that she hadn't thought to bring her mascara wand along to the party, not anticipating that she was going to be indulging in floods of tears before the evening was out.

Sebastian, on the watch for them, threaded quickly

through the crowd to Roxanne's side, and asked, 'Everything okay?'

'Yes.' She hooked her arm in Delia's and said, 'We seem to have lost our drinks. Think you can manage to rustle some more up for us?'

He looked at Delia with veiled curiosity, smiled down at her reassuringly, and said, 'Bacardi and Coke, wasn't it?' She nodded, and he said,' There's a nice wide chair over there, just vacated by a very large lady. I'm sure you two girls could share it.'

Gratefully, Delia sat in the chair, while Roxanne perched protectively on the arm. Max was circulating, keeping the party going, but he took one long, expressionless look at them and kept away from their corner. Another man asked Delia to dance, and when she refused, shaking her head, he tugged at her hand, saying, 'Aw, come on, Delia—be a sport!'

'No, thanks, Harry,' she said, pulling vainly against his hold, and then Sebastian came up and said crisply, 'The lady said no!' He gave Delia her drink, and Harry met his level stare and melted away, looking mystified.

He wasn't the only one. The threesome of Delia, Roxanne and Sebastian was an obvious cause of curiosity and speculation. When Roxanne said to Sebastian, 'Can we go soon? And we could drop Delia on our way, couldn't we?' Sebastian agreed as though it was the most natural thing in the world. But the stares increased as the three of them stood in the doorway to thank Max and say goodnight. And Max gave them a hard look and said, 'I'll take Delia home.'

Delia shrank against Roxanne, and Sebastian shot a look at her and said, 'No need, Max. She'll be quite safe with us.'

Max's face went grim, and darkened with colour. 'She'd be perfectly safe with me, as a matter of fact,' he said.

'Of course she would,' Roxanne agreed quickly. 'But she's tired, and you can't leave your guests yet. Thanks for a lovely party.'

'Oh, sure,' Max said sourly. His eyes went to the girl at her side, and he said distinctly, 'Goodnight, Delia.'

'Goodnight, Max,' she murmured without looking at him.

Max made an exasperated sound and turned away as they went out into the cool night.

CHAPTER SIX

ROXANNE was grateful that Sebastian had to spend much of his time in Auckland. She saw him at weekends, but seldom in between, and most of the time she managed to avoid being alone with him.

Her father was looking much more relaxed these days, and also spending a good deal of time in Auckland. Roxanne gathered that the negotiations were proceeding satisfactorily.

One Friday afternoon Sebastian arrived in the shop at mid-afternoon, as she was inspecting some carvings which old Mr Ihaka and Herena Kahi had brought in for her to sell.

The old man and his pupil greeted Sebastian with pleasure, and Herena shyly congratulated him. Mr Ihaka gave him a gleaming look and said, 'They reckon you're a demon with the women. Two at once, eh?'

Looking astonished, and then rueful, Sebastian said firmly, 'No, only one, Mr Ihaka. For the rest of my life.'

The old man nodded, looking brightly at Roxanne, and handing her one of the smaller carvings from the bulging flax kit he had brought them in. 'That's the ticket!' he said, turning to Sebastian again. 'My great-grandfather, you know, he had two wives. But too much trouble, eh? That's no good—two women wanting the same man all the time. Nothing but trouble.'

Sebastian shot a look at Roxanne that held a glint of laughter, and said gravely, 'I'm sure you're right, Mr Ihaka. I'll bear it in mind.'

Roxanne hid a smile, and bent her head to examine the carved *mere* that he was holding. Her fingers ran along the curved wooden blade of the short hand-weapon, and Herena said with soft laughter, 'I think Roxanne might have something to say about that, anyway.'

'Mm. Perhaps I'll take charge of *that*!' said Sebastian, neatly removing the *mere* from Roxanne's grasp.

They all laughed and, looking into Sebastian's smiling eyes, Roxanne woke up with sudden shock to the fact that somewhere along the way she had learned to like him very much—and that what she was planning to do to him was mean and despicable.

Her hand shook as she took a carved figure of a warrior from Herena, and examined it without seeing it all. She couldn't go on deceiving Sebastian, she thought with horror. She would have to put an end to the farce, and apologise for leading him on. Watching his face as he smiled down at Herena and complimented her on the intricate carving of the warrior's feathered cloak, she thought what an idiot she had been. She should have been honest from the beginning—he wasn't inhuman, after all. He could be remarkably gentle and understanding.

But she needed privacy to make her confession to him. There was none in the shop, and very little at the Challis house. In the event, it was Sunday before she got the chance to speak to him alone, without fear of interruption. And then she found it not as easy to broach the subject. He had driven her out to his house, and as he opened the door for her, he said 'Come into my parlour——'

She tried to smile, shaking her head as she walked past him, into the room which seemed dim after the bright sunshine outside.

Behind her, he said, 'I've been dying to get you alone,' and turned her into his arms.

Roxanne couldn't avoid his kiss, but her misery and nervousness must have communicated itself to him, and after a few moments he lifted his mouth from hers, rested his cheek on her hair and said, 'What's the matter, love?'

She couldn't tell him like this, nestled in his arms. She pulled away from him, and he let her go reluctantly, frowning.

Her vision clearing, she turned to look out the long windows facing the sea. 'I've got something to tell you.' she started stiltedly.

'That sounds ominous.' He came and slipped an arm about her waist, trying to see her face. But Roxanne looked away.

'Sebastian, I can't marry you,' she said baldly.

He didn't move. She felt the arm behind her tense, but the warm weight of his hand on her waist didn't change. Quite calmly, he asked, 'Why not?'

'I—it was all a mistake,' she said huskily. 'I'm terribly sorry, Sebastian. I've been a fool, and—and a cheat, I suppose. I should never have become engaged to you. I haven't been honest——'

He said, 'You mean it was really Mark, all along.'

'Mark?' She looked up at him then, and saw that his face was hard and unreadable, his eyes darkly opaque. 'No,' she said, 'it isn't Mark. It was—because of the merger my father wanted.'

His hands took her shoulders and made her face him. 'Let me get this straight,' he said. 'You agreed to marry me to make sure the merger went through?'

'Yes,' she whispered unhappily. 'I—never meant to marry you, really. But please try to understand. My father was worried sick, and when you asked me, I couldn't see any other way. I'm sorry.'

'You're sorry,' he repeated, and she saw the deep, frightening anger in his eyes and tried to move out of his grasp.

'I *am*,' she said. 'Truly I am. I don't blame you for being angry, but——'

'But now that the agreements on the merger are safely signed and sealed, you want out!' said Sebastian grimly

'Oh, are they?' she said. 'I didn't know.'

'Didn't you?' he drawled sarcastically, making her flinch. 'Surely Daddy told you that the plan had worked out?'

She went cold. 'My father knows nothing about any—plan,' she said. 'This was all my own idea.'

Sebastian took his hands from her shoulders, and only then she realised how tightly he had gripped her, there was a numbing ache where his fingers had been.

'Oh, yes?' he sneered, thrusting his hands into his pockets, as though he couldn't trust himself to keep them from her throat. 'He only threw you at me every opportunity out of the goodness of his heart?'

Her cheeks warmed uncomfortably. 'He didn't do anything of the kind——'

'Of course he did. He saw at once that I found you attractive, and he played on it for all he was worth. Don't tell me he didn't ask you to be *nice* to me!'

She couldn't say that he hadn't, of course. But she said spiritedly, 'All right, so he did. But he also said I wasn't to make any extravagant sacrifices!'

'Like marrying me, for real?'

'That's right! He thought our engagement was genuine, just as everyone else did.'

'Including me! Well, you certainly obeyed instructions, didn't you? You haven't sacrificed a thing! You must think you've been clever.'

'I didn't mean to hurt you, Sebastian, believe me. You don't know how badly my father's business had been going lately . . .'

'It didn't take me long to find out. And let me tell you, if it hadn't been for you, the merger would never have taken place. Congratulations!'

'Don't! I've said I'm desperately sorry——'

Fiery
Passion.
Forbidden
Love.
Free.
A Contemporary Love Story
LOVE BEYOND DESIRE
RACHEL PALMER
...At his touch,
her body felt a
familiar wild stir-
ring, but she
struggled to
resist it. This is
not love, she
thought bitterly.

'Yes, you have. What comes next? Goodbye, and no hard feelings? Or do you hope we'll always be friends? That might be the best line, considering your father is now a business partner of mine—or so you imagine.'

'What do you mean by that?' Roxanne asked quickly, alarmed.

Sebastian smiled, in a distinctly unamused fashion, and said, 'There are certain legal formalities that are not quite complete. I bet Neal can find a dozen little loopholes to get me out of that contract, and leave your darling daddy high and dry. You've jumped the gun, my sweet. You shouldn't have been in such a hurry to renege on your part of the bargain.'

'You wouldn't——! Look, I told you it has nothing to do with my father! And there was no bargain, you know that——!'

'On the contrary, I think there was. Admittedly you kept me in the dark about your real intentions, but if you expect me to honour the merger, you will damn well honour your promise to me!'

'Marry you?' she asked blankly. 'You can't hold me to that!'

'Can't I? Do *you* know just how badly your father needs his business propping up? I doubt he could hold on another three weeks, without Renners.'

'If you knew, didn't it ever occur to you that—that I might have accepted your proposal for—well, for other than the usual reasons?'

'It did—once. And I dismissed the idea as absurd—and insulting to you.'

Roxanne saw the cynical downturn of his mouth when he said that, and she went pale. 'I'm sorry if I've disillusioned you,' she said.

'Stop saying you're sorry!' he said harshly. 'Life is full of disillusionments. At least I know now what I'll be getting, don't I?'

'A reluctant wife? You don't really want that, surely?'

Coldly, he said, 'Nobody makes a fool of me, Roxanne. And nobody walks out on an agreement with me. I've told you what will happen—and don't kid yourself that I didn't mean it.'

'You're not really in love with me, are you?' she said. 'You're determined to hold me to this for revenge.'

'Revenge? Nothing so melodramatic. It suits me to marry you, and if you have some romantic idea that if I really loved you I'd let you go free, think again. I'm no knight in shining armour. I'm a man, and I want you, and I'm not letting you get away with leading me up the garden path and thinking that now you've got what you wanted, you can just calmly walk out on me. You've picked the wrong guy for that.'

'If I don't—carry it through,' she said, 'you'll ruin my father?'

'That's right.' He was immovable, and she had no doubt that he meant it. All vestige of softness and humour had gone from his face. He was an adversary, dangerous and determined. He wasn't bluffing.

'How can you?' she said, inwardly trembling. 'You'll make me hate you—what can you get out of that?'

Sebastian slid his gaze over her with deliberate, blatant insult, and she clenched her hands and turned away from him. It was answer enough, but it frightened and sickened her. There was no tenderness in his eyes now, and no smile. This was not the man she had begun to like almost too much, the amusing, considerate companion who made her laugh and taught her to respond to his passion with a trustful abandonment. This was a stranger who looked at her with an angry contempt, and whose eyes held only naked desire and a determination to take what he wanted, regardless of her feelings.

'You won't hate me,' he said with quiet confidence.

Defiantly, Roxanne swung round to look at him, her eyes angry. 'I will, if you try and force me——'

'The choice is yours. I'm just pointing out that you don't get something for nothing. Not from me.'

'My father said once,' she said slowly, 'that you were first and foremost a businessman. I shouldn't have forgotten that.'

'No, you shouldn't.'

'Do you think of everything in debits and credits? You have to get value for your money, even out of human relationships?'

'You were the one who got engaged for the sake of business, Roxanne. *You* set the terms. All I ask is that you stand by them. They're simple enough: marriage in return for the merger. No marriage, no merger.'

She chewed on her lip uncertainly. This was a nightmare, surely, too fantastic to be true. 'I—can't——' she faltered.

Sebastian shrugged. 'I didn't realise I was so repulsive,' he said. 'You must be a very good actress. You'd better tell your father it's all off—or shall I?'

He moved as thought to show her out, and Roxanne put out a hand and caught at his sleeve. 'Sebastian—please! You'd break him—and my mother, too. I thought you were growing fond of her, and Rhonda . . .'

'You know the price, Roxanne.'

She drew back from him. 'Of their happiness and peace of mind? The sacrifice of mine, you mean.' She drew in a quick, hard breath. 'All right, Sebastian, I'll pay your price. I only hope you find it's worth it.'

Something unreadable glittered in his eyes, and he said, 'Oh, I think it will be. Let's seal the new agreement, shall we?'

He reached for her, and she stood stiffly in the circle of his arms as he kissed her, her lips unresponsive and cool. He drew back for an instant and looked at the deliberate contempt in her face, and his mouth hardened. He tipped her head back in his hands and kissed her angrily, uncaring if he hurt her, and her hands went up against his chest in protest, then curled into fists beating against his shoulders and upper arms.

Unexpectedly, he swung her off her feet and, still kissing her, strode into the bedroom and lowered her to the black silk cover, coming after her to imprison her with his body.

Startled and furious, Roxanne wrenched away her mouth, flailing ineffectually at him with a hand that was quickly caught and held. Her voice high with fright, she demanded, 'What the hell do you think you're doing?'

'Collecting something on account.' Sebastian's mouth descended on hers again, implacable, sensuous and hard. Her struggles were useless, and with growing dismay she found that not only could she not escape the muscled body that held her down, the hands that held her wrists, and the kiss that was ravaging the softness of her mouth; her own body was turning traitor, and urging her to give in, tiny wavelets of pleasure forcing their way into her consciousness, trickling inexorably over her skin, a sudden rocketing of desire making her quiver when he licked softly at her lips, and then the hollow behind her ear, then let his mouth glide to the deeper hollow at her throat, covering it while his tongue found the pulse in the warm cleft.

Alarmed, she made a panicky little sound, half sob, half sigh, and tears burned between her tightly closed lids.

His mouth left her, and she turned her head away, trying to hide the tears. One of her hands was freed, and his fingers touched her face. 'Roxanne,' he said. She tried to move her head, but he wouldn't let her. 'Roxanne!' His voice was thickened, but imperative.

She opened her eyes, the tears arrested. Sebastian was looking down at her with eyes as brilliant and hard as diamonds. 'Are you really a virgin?' he asked her roughly. 'Or was that part of the act, too?'

Her eyes darkened as she stared back at him. She tried to shake her head, said, 'Yes, I am.'

She felt his muscles tense, and he drew a deep, harsh breath. Then he shifted away from her and stood up. His gaze slid over her hotly, and she realised that her skirt had ridden up her thighs, and her hair was dishevelled about her face. 'I need a swim,' he said. 'I'll see you on the beach.'

Roxanne heard him leave the house, and got up shakily off the bed, automatically straightening the cover before she left the bedroom. In the kitchen she turned on the cold tap, splashed her face and dried it with a paper towel, then poured herself a drink of water, wishing vaguely for something stronger, but unwilling to use Sebastian's liquor—a strange little scruple, she admitted wryly to herself.

She didn't go down to the beach, but sat waiting for him on the terrace, pretending to read a magazine while an irritating breeze kept flapping the pages.

When he came back he was still wet from the sea, a towel slung about his neck, brief swimming trunks emphasising his masculine physique.

Barely glancing at her, he went inside, and ten minutes later came out wearing light casual hip-hugging pants and an open shirt. He handed her a glass, and she sipped at gin and lime as he sank into a chair opposite and said, 'The water's fine. Don't you fancy it?'

Roxanne shook her head and took another sip, not looking at him.

He had a glass, too, from which he drank without apparent pleasure. She watched the gulls sailing purposefully against the bright sky, and the pale glitter of the sun on the distant ripples of the sea. A fantail chirped somewhere in the trees nearby, and a fat native wood-pigeon whirred heavily across her vision in a flash of white and cerise and grey.

Sebastian put down his empty glass on the flagstones beside his chair, and said, 'We're not going to spend the rest of our engagement in a frozen silence, are we?'

Nursing her glass between her hands, her eyes on the half inch of liquid left, she said in a low voice, 'What do you want me to say?'

'How about, "I love you"?' he suggested sarcastically. 'Or, "Darling, I can't wait until our wedding day"? Neither would be true, of course, but you lie so sweetly . . .'

'Stop it!' she exclaimed, rising quickly from her chair. He got up, too, and as she turned from him, with a blind instinct to flee, he put out his hand and caught her arm, so roughly that her glass fell to the stones under their feet and smashed, and Sebastian jerked her out of its way, his fingers hard on her shoulders, holding her.

Her palms were against his shirt, his chin close to her temple. She looked at the rise and fall of his chest, between the open edges of his shirt, and said, 'That isn't fair. I didn't lie to you.'

'You lied by implication,' he argued, 'when you let me think you wanted to marry me. You lied every time you kissed me and let me hold you like this . . .'

His arms came round her, moulding her soft shape to his. Trying to escape. Roxanne curled her hands into fists, pushing against him.

'No, not like that,' he said softly, and his fingers prised hers cruelly open and pressed them hard against his skin. 'Touch me,' he muttered. 'Go on, Roxanne. Tell me some more of your sweet lies.'

'No——' she moaned as his mouth sought hers in a punitive, violent kiss that bent her head back and bruised her lips. Her back arched as he held her against him, and she felt his ribs against her palms, knew the quickened rhythm of his breathing.

She was shaking when he eased his hold on her, looking down at her with glittering, disturbing anger and passion. 'Please,' she whispered. 'Please take me home, Sebastian. I—c-can't take any more today.'

For a moment there was cruelty in his face, and her heart sank as she wondered what further punishment he had in store for her. But when she made a futile little gesture of submission, her head falling forward as her shoulders drooped in his hold, Sebastian said curtly, 'All right, I'll take you home.'

She stumbled as he turned her with his hand on her arm, and he said, 'You're not going to faint on me, are you?' His voice taunted harshly, without compassion.

Roxanne shook her head. She must be pale, she supposed. She felt exhausted and weepy. But she wouldn't cry again, not in front of him. All the liking that had begun to grow for him had evaporated. She felt the old antagonism flooding back, and with it a new, helpless emotion of stark fear.

The fear didn't leave her in the next weeks before the wedding. Now that it was a reality, it seemed to be coming closer with the speed of light. And nothing she could do was going to keep it at bay. Sebastian was all urbanity and easy teasing when they were with her family, but away from them the teasing took on a malicious edge, and his kisses were very nearly brutal. She was glad that during the week she didn't see him, but the weekends were a distinct strain. The last Sunday before the wedding date he took her for a drive and on the way home drew into a shadowed grassy area beneath a stand of silver-leafed beech, and pulled her into his arms.

Roxanne let him kiss her unresistingly, her reactions dulled with fatigue and the knowledge that there was no escape from the retribution he had planned for her. It would be better if she could feel nothing, not even the angry resentment that sometimes stiffened her body against him, until his mouth and his hands exacted a reluctant submission.

Her lack of resistance made him more gentle this time, his mouth wandering from hers to glide over her skin as though he loved the taste of it, and his hands shaping her face and shoulders, going down to her thighs and back to her waist. When they touched her breasts, exploringly, she stirred, protesting, and he moved away, but after a moment she realised that his fingers were slowly undoing the buttons of her blouse, and she grabbed at his wrists, digging in her nails to stop him, to drag his hands away.

He did stop, but his hands stayed where they were, his thumbs pushing aside the material, stroking the skin beneath, while his fingers spread over her breasts, outside the blouse.

'Stop it!' she said, between her teeth.

'No—let me——' His lips were on her throat, moving down, his hands insistent.

'*No!*' She pushed him away strongly, and when his head came up and his arms tried to drag her closer again, she slapped him.

For a moment she saw murder in his eyes. Then he let her go quite suddenly, and laughed, without much humour. 'Your wedding nerves are showing, darling,' he said. 'You won't slap me next week.'

'You don't *own* me *yet*!' she snapped, furiously doing up her blouse.

'Own you? Is that how you view marriage?' His voice was harsh and angry.

'This marriage, yes. You've bought me at the price of my father's company, haven't you? But possession date is next Saturday. Until then, keep your hands off the merchandise, will you?'

He leaned back in the seat, half turned to face her, a satirical smile on his lips. 'If you insist.' His eyes still glittered with suppressed rage.

'I do!'

Inclining his dark head ironically, Sebastian said softly, 'Do you hate me, Roxanne?'

'Yes.' The monosyllable came out flat, uncompromising.

'Well,' he said, and his fingers just brushed her cheek, her hair, before he withdrew them, 'we'll have to see what we can do about that—after next Saturday.'

Delia had offered to do Roxanne's hair, free, on her wedding morning. Roxanne had included her in the invitation list, in spite of Mrs Challis's raised eyebrows.

She arranged Roxanne's hair for her in a variation of her usual style, combed into a chignon, but with pretty tendrils allowed to frame her face under the circlet of artificial daisies that held the lacy, traditional veil. Putting the finishing touches to it, after Roxanne had donned the long-sleeved, heavy silk gown, Delia stood back and surveyed her with satisfaction mixed with awe and admiration. 'You look stunning! You'll knock him dead when you walk up the aisle!'

Roxanne's laugher was hollow. That would solve a lot of problems, she thought with grim humour, but it wasn't likely to happen. She turned to look in the full length mirror at herself, and for a moment caught her breath. The dress was beautiful. In spite of herself, she had wanted to look lovely on her wedding day, and it had been chosen with care. She looked pale and her eyes were very blue, the pupils enlarged mysteriously, the misty veil adding to her appearance a fragile look that was not at all her everyday self. From that moment reality began to recede, and she accepted without really noticing that the arrangements they had made were proceeding like clockwork, and found herself standing in the church porch, then gliding down the aisle on her father's arm, with no very clear idea how she had got there.

She recited the rehearsed words obediently with the tall grim stranger at her side, and it was only when he pushed the gold circlet on to her finger that she looked up and saw his dark eyes strangely intent on her face.

At that instant time stood still, and she thought, I've promised to love him and honour him, until death do us part, and he's promised, too. But he doesn't honour me, he despises me, and I don't love him—do I?

The question hovered at the edge of her mind, but the service was going on, and she listened to the words that were being intoned over them. They were solemn words, this was a solemn, irrevocable thing that they were doing. For all the wrong reasons, she thought, and bowed her head, praying that somehow things might be made right. Then it was time to sign the register, and receive the congratulations of her family.

Her mother's cheeks were wet, but Rhonda, pretty and vivid in her bridesmaid's dress of autumn colours printed on silk chiffon, was sparkling as she kissed her sister and insisted on doing the same for Sebastian. Roxanne felt a pang of envy as she saw his face soften for Rhonda, but when he turned to her she dared not meet his eyes, afraid of what she might see in them. She had closed her eyes when he lowered his lips briefly and coolly to hers, standing rigid in the circle of his arms, thinking only that the family must not know how matters really were between them.

In the car on the short journey to the reception he held her hand in a hard grip, his eyes on the ring which he had placed on her finger. Roxanne, glancing at his face, could not see his eyes, and his mouth looked straight and firm, with no sign of softness.

At the reception she sat beside him, and listened without hearing much to the toasts and speeches, smiling indiscriminately and longing for it all to be over.

She noticed that her father was in jovial spirits, and at one stage saw Max Ansell making his way purposefully to where Delia was standing with a couple of admiring young men. Delia had acquired a new touch of elegance, with a shorter, sleeker hairstyle, and was wearing a blue dress that matched her eyes and did things for her figure without being too blatant about it. She still wore rather a lot of make-up, but she had toned it down somewhat to go with the blue. Roxanne thought she looked very pretty, and although she was sparkling for the young men, she kept her hands firmly anchored on the glass in them, and her laughter was subdued.

Forgetting her own problems for a few moments, Roxanne watched with interest as Max planted himself firmly by Delia's side and spoke to her. She saw the girl's look of surprise, and the cool, firm shake of her head, and although Max had his back to her, so that his expression was invisible, Roxanne saw quite clearly the sudden reddening of his neck, before he turned abruptly away. The main part of the reception was over, and her mother was gathering up the family to return to the house. People milled about, offering each other lifts, deciding whether to accept the general invitation to continue the party at the Challis home, or to call it a day. When next Roxanne saw Max he was leaning on a pillar, broodingly drinking from a glass of whisky, and watching Delia who was departing on the arm of one of the young men she had been talking to.

On impulse, Roxanne left Sebastian talking to an elderly aunt of her mother's, and went over to Max. He saw her coming and straightened, giving her a wary, mocking smile. 'You're a beautiful bride, Roxanne,' he said, kissing her boldly on her mouth. 'Sebastian's a lucky man.'

'Thank you. Do you know where Delia's got to? She did my hair for me, and I wanted to give her one of the roses off the wedding cake, for a memento. Didn't I see you talking to her, earlier?'

His jaded eyes regarded her ironically. 'You saw me getting the brush-off,' he said. 'She's gone off with some young colleague of your husband's. Probably for a night on the town. No doubt she'll persuade him to help her paint it a suitable shade of red.'

'I doubt that,' she said calmly. 'Delia's quietened down a lot lately. Haven't you noticed?'

With deliberate cynicism he said, 'Don't worry, it won't last. She's just found something new in trousers, and the minute she saw him she was back to her old tricks.'

'Is that what you said to her just now?'

'In front of the new heartthrob? Give me credit! I offered her a lift home. She said no. Finish.'

'You hurt her a lot, you know,' said Roxanne.

'She's had it coming.'

'I take it *your* morals will stand any amount of examination?' Roxanne asked crisply.

Max had the grace to look slightly shamed. 'Okay,' he said. 'Point taken. I came down too hard on her. I lost my temper.'

'Why?' Roxanne asked softly.

'You know why,' he answered. 'I'd been wanting to wring her silly little neck for months, but I never realised why until that night at my party—and then I blew it. She's never going to speak to me again—and when I'm capable of thinking logically, I don't blame her. She must hate me.'

'I don't think people make drastic changes in themselves to please someone they hate, do you?' Roxanne asked thoughtfully.

For a moment a glimmer of hope showed in his eyes. Then he shook his head and said, 'I just made her see herself the way others see her, that's all. She certainly isn't doing anything to please *me*.'

'Not consciously,' Roxanne admitted. 'But she must have some—some regard for your opinion. She *has* changed, Max, quite markedly. She even thought of letting her hair go mouse and wearing clothes that she hates. I had to talk her out of sackcloth and ashes.'

'The little idiot!' he said, with a faint smile, and the look in his eyes was one she had never seen there before. 'Trust Delia to go the whole hog.'

'She *is* like that,' Roxanne agreed. 'If you're not careful, she'll end up in a convent.'

For a moment he looked bemused, then he shouted with laughter. 'We can't have that!' he said. Then sobering, he added, 'But if she wanted to, *I* couldn't stop her.'

'I think you might. I'll tell you one thing—if she ever fell really in love, I think he'd be a very lucky guy. As you say, she doesn't do anything by halves.'

Max looked away from her, and she knew that he wasn't seeing the crowded room about them at all. In his face there was sudden hunger, stark and unmistakable, and then the look faded and his eyes returned to her face, holding bitter hopelessness. 'She won't even see me!'

'Look, you both live in the same town,' Roxanne pointed out. 'She can't help seeing you, in a casual way. Sooner or later you'll get an opportunity for a few minutes with her, alone. But watch your temper, Max. She's afraid of men, you know.'

'*Afraid?*'

'Yes. She told me. They're bigger and stronger, and when a man's in a temper, the only way she knows to cope with it is to wheedle him out of it.'

Roxanne saw him recalling with something like shock the events at his house when he had taken Delia away from the party into the bedroom. Remembering Delia in their schooldays, her timid mother, and her father who had died when Delia was seventeen, she said softly, 'I have an idea that Delia's father's ideas on discipline were pretty—primitive.'

Max wasn't slow at putting two and two together. His jaw tight, he said, 'I see. And I scared her out of her mind.' He paused. 'That stupid little-girl act of hers!'

'Maybe it's not entirely an act.'

'No.' He burst out, 'She always looks so damned *sexy*! And underneath it all, she's such a baby!' He sounded exasperated beyond endurance, and Roxanne smiled sympathetically. 'She's got no more sense than a two-year-old!' Max finished.

'You're still angry with her, aren't you?'

'Yes, dammit, I am! No—no, not with her. I'm mad with myself—I'm thirty-one and I've never felt like this in my life before. And now—now it has to be a girl like Delia!'

Roxanne eyed him thoughtfully. 'You wouldn't hurt her again, would you, Max? What—exactly—do you want?'

His lip curled in self-derision, he said, 'It's all right, Roxanne. Believe it or not, I want to persuade the silly bitch to marry me. And after that I'll keep her on a very short string. If she so much as flutters one of those preposterous eyelashes of hers, it had better be at me!'

He sounded impossibly chauvinistic and possessive, but Roxanne thought that very likely Delia would find a great sense of security in a jealous husband who made it clear he would allow no straying. All the same, it promised to be a stormy relationship.

'Well, good luck to you,' she shrugged. And Max, suddenly reverting to gloom, said sourly, 'Thanks, I'll need it.'

Sebastian joined them, saying to Roxanne, 'Your mother says it's time we left.'

'Yes,' she said. 'I'm coming.' The interlude with

Max seemed to have brought reality back, and she was sharply aware now of Sebastian's hand on her waist, of the disturbing, unreadable glitter in his eyes.

They left from the house an hour later, in Sebastian's car which Neal Osborne had produced from some hiding place at the appointed time. They were heading for Auckland and the airport, where they would board a plane for Rotorua. When Sebastian had asked her where she wanted to spend their honeymoon, Roxanne had suggested the resort with near-sarcasm, and he had tightened his mouth and taken her at her word. They were booked into one of the city's largest hotels, near the thermal area of Whakarewarewa.

'You seem very well organised,' she said. 'Did you and Neal synchronise your watches?'

'We're old partners in crime,' Sebastian said. 'Going back to our student days.'

'Well, we don't appear to be trailing any old shoes, and I think I foiled my sister's plans to fill my suitcase with confetti, by keeping the key well hidden.'

With an absent smile, he said, 'I should think Rhonda is a very resourceful young woman. I wouldn't count on having foiled her, if I were you.'

For a time he drove in silence, and she felt tension gathering. 'Your mother looks very youthful,' she said. Mrs Blair had been charming to her, but in a slightly cool way. Roxanne found her very much like her letter.

Sebastian shrugged, and said, 'So is yours.'

'It—it all went off very well, don't you think?'

'Very well. Your mother is to be congratulated.'

'Are you being sarcastic?' she asked, mindful of a harsh note in his voice.

'No. But you don't have to indulge in small talk for my benefit, Roxanne.'

She lapsed into silence, and looked out of the side window, blinking hard to dispel quick, dismaying tears. Sebastian drove on for a few miles, then asked suddenly, 'Are you sulking?'

'No.'

But she didn't look at him, and he threw her a look and then drew up in the shade of a patch of macrocarpa trees, on the grass verge. A bunch of sheep which had been grazing close to the road scattered and ran, their white rumps bobbing ridiculously, but she didn't smile.

Sebastian's long fingers closed on her chin and turned her face to him. 'Scared?' he said.

Her mouth closed stubbornly, and her lashes fluttered down to hide her eyes. That was a mistake, because a tear escaped on to her cheek, and he raised his other hand and flicked at it with one finger.

'I won't rape you, Roxanne,' he promised softly. 'Does that help?'

Her teeth descended on her lower lip, hard. Still with her eyes averted, she said, 'Why did you insist on marrying me?'

After a long silence he said, 'I thought I'd already explained that.'

'Because you don't like being cheated out of a bargain?'

'There's also—this,' he said, and kissed her, a long, seeking, explicit kiss that made her heart pound and left her gasping.

But she hadn't kissed him back, and when he lifted his mouth from hers at last, and looked down at her flushed face, there was frustration and anger in his eyes. He let her go and started the car again in silence.

He was annoyed that he had failed to draw a response from her. Roxanne guessed that he expected to be able to arouse her so that there was no need for him to use force. That was all his promise had meant. Only he wasn't going to find it so easy. Something in her rebelled at the prospect of a loveless coming together, based on sexual instinct and nothing else. If Sebastian had ever loved her, his feelings had apparently died abruptly when he discovered that she had been intending to cheat him. Now he only wanted his pound of flesh. And his hard, remorseless pursuit of the debt she owed had stifled the first stirring of love she had begun to feel for him, that had led to her disastrously honest confession. He blamed her for her lack of integrity, and she blamed him for his lack of understanding. And what kind of marriage could be built on resentment and disillusion, and bitterness? What chance did they have for any sort of lasting happiness?

CHAPTER SEVEN

THEY had dinner at the hotel, and Roxanne discovered to her surprise that she was hungry enough to do full justice to succulent Bluff oysters, a lamb casserole redolent of wine and herbs, and a dessert of fluffy pavlova topped with kiwi-fruit and cream. A light sparkling wine accompanied the meal, and the coffee afterwards was strong and aromatic. The hotel had a small dance floor and a three-piece orchestra was playing, but Roxanne shook her head when Sebastian asked her if she wanted to dance. She didn't want to be held close to him, swaying to romantic music on a dimly lit and pocket-size dance floor.

When he got up and pulled out her chair for her, she realised that the privacy of their room with its twin beds and two armchairs would be almost as intimate, and said quickly, 'I'd like some fresh air. Can we go for a walk?'

'Sure. Will you be warm enough?'

She was wearing a skirt and jacket over a natural silk blouse. She nodded, and they went out of the dining room and through the lobby into the cool night.

Sebastian drawled, 'Fresh air, did you say?' And she laughed, because the smell of sulphur was thick and pungent.

'It's supposed to be healthy,' she reminded him. 'Anyway, you soon get used to it.'

He took her arm, guiding her around a cairn of stones at the side of the path, where steam issued forth in lazy jets, and the bubbling of subterranean boiling water carried to their ears.

'Definitely a place to stick to the straight and narrow

when walking at night,' he said.

About to agree, Roxanne closed her mouth on the light rejoinder. He was being nice, deliberately so, hoping to lower her guard. His hand on her arm was firmly possessive, his thumb beginning a light, stroking caress as he strolled beside her, matching his stride to hers.

Roxanne moved her arm out of his hold, unmistakably rejecting. Sebastian didn't stop her, but she felt his annoyance as he quickened his pace a little, thrusting both hands into his trouser pockets.

They walked on in silence for some time, until they reached the public gardens that lay on the shore of the lake, and took one of the broad paths that led to the water. Moonlight rippled over the surface, and wavelets slapped quietly against the narrow white shore, while the scent of roses mingled with the pervading smell of sulphur. On an ornamental bridge spanning a tiny hot stream spilling into the cold waters of the lake, Sebastian suddenly stopped, his arm going in front of Roxanne to place his hand on the wooden railing.

She turned from him, facing the lake, both of her own hands gripping the wood before her. She could feel his breath in her hair, the warmth of his chest at her back. Somewhere not far away, a Maori concert was going on. She could hear the blended voices, the rhythmic thump of bare feet stamping on boards. Closer at hand was the sound of Sebastian's breathing, light and even, and her own, that had quickened with apprehension.

His finger flicked at a tendril of her hair lying on her neck, and she felt his lips teasing at her nape, and shivered. His arms slid about her, his hands just under her breasts, drawing her to him.

'Relax,' he said against her earlobe. 'Enjoy the view and the moonlight.' His mouth withdrew, and he stood holding her against him. She put her hands on his, trying to prise them off, but he took no notice, and she knew he wasn't going to. Anger flared briefly, but she was suddenly very tired, too tired to fight him. Gradually she did as he had suggested, relaxed against the warmth and strength of his body, and when one of his hands began a light, insidious, stroking exploration of her breast, her waist, her hip and stomach, she didn't stir. Through her half-closed eyes, the shimmering moon-glazed water began to assume a hypnotic quality, and the sweetly tantalising caress was giving her a dreamy pleasure.

When his hand moved lower to hold her to him in a more intimate way, the pleasure intensified, shocking her into awareness, and her head went back suddenly against his shoulder as she uttered a low cry that was half protest and half bewildered delight.

He turned her in his arms and sought her mouth, shattering the dream in a storm of unleashed passion. Her head was pressed back into the curve of his shoulder, his arms held her so closely she could feel the hard beating of his heart, the deep, fast rise and fall of his chest as he breathed against her softly crushed breasts, and the hot, urgent desire that was having its inevitable effect on his body.

It was that which frightened her back to some semblance of sanity, after a few moments of blind, instinctive response. She began to fight him, making sounds of muted protest against the demands of his mouth, pushing her hands against his shoulders.

Sebastian took his mouth reluctantly from hers, but did not release her. 'Don't, you little idiot,' he said huskily. 'Don't fight me. There's nothing to be frightened of.'

'That's easy for you to say!' she said fiercely. 'What do you *expect*, when you're using brute force to hold me—to kiss me?'

For a moment longer he held her, looking down at

the dim blur of her face in the moonlight. Then he let her go and stepped back, ostentatiously putting a foot of space between them. 'There you are,' he said. 'The brute has let you go. Shall we get back to the hotel?'

In their room, he asked if she wanted the bathroom first, and she accepted, gathering up her nightgown and its matching nylon satin robe, both a deep, smoky pink trimmed with wide lace edgings.

She took a long time in the shower, brushed her hair with long, hard strokes before leaving the bathroom, and emerged with the robe firmly belted about her slim waist.

Sebastian had discarded his jacket and unbuttoned his shirt. He looked her over unsmilingly as she walked past him, then he picked up a dark silk robe that was lying on one of the beds and went into the bathroom.

Roxanne didn't see any pyjamas, and when he came back into the bedroom a scant ten minutes later, she knew he was wearing nothing under the loosely belted robe. She was sitting on one of the beds leafing through a magazine, and when he came and stood before her, his feet planted apart on the light coloured carpet, she looked up defiantly into his eyes.

He took the magazine from her and put it on the table between the beds.

'Still hating me, Roxanne? he asked softly.

His eyes mocked her, and with an uprush of antagonism, she said baldly, 'Yes.'

'That's a pity.' He reached down unhurriedly and grasped her hands, pulling her to her feet. Still holding one of her wrists, he released the other to grasp the covers of the bed behind her and draw them back. Then his hand tugged at the satin belt that held her robe, until its edges parted and he slipped it off her shoulders.

'Very nice,' he murmured, his fingers touching the snowy lace border over her breasts. 'Very virginal.'

He pushed her down on to the bed quite gently, bent to swing her feet up from the floor, then dropped the covers over her.

'Goodnight, sweet wife,' he said, smiling knowingly down into her astonished face, and switched off the lamp.

In the morning when she woke, he was already dressed, sitting on the other bed and reading the morning paper.

'Hello,' he said, as she looked at him warily. 'Breakfast starts in ten minutes, and I've arranged a rental car for nine o'clock. Any particular place you'd like to go?'

Roxanne shook her head mutely.

He cast her a keen look, and said blandly, 'There are plenty of interesting places. I've been looking at some of the brochures the management kindly provides. Have you been to the Buried Village?'

'When I was a child,' she said.

'Fancy it?'

'Do you?'

Sebastian stood up suddenly, and she just managed not to cringe. From her present position he looked very tall, and very mediaeval, like an inquisitor. 'I'm trying to please you, my lady wife,' he said. 'It *was* your idea to come here.'

'You know perfectly well I didn't care! I didn't want a honeymoon at all.'

'You didn't even want a wedding, did you?' he said tauntingly. 'But you got one, anyway. And now you're having a honeymoon, just like in the storybooks. Kisses in the moonlight last night, and the pleasures of sightseeing today. Or would you prefer to spend the day here—that's also in the honeymoon tradition, of course.'

'I certainly don't want to stay here with you!' she

flashed. Throwing back the covers, she grabbed for her robe and pulled it on as she stood up. 'You're the lord and master—we'll go wherever you want, of course! Personally, I've always hated this place, it gives me the creeps!'

The weather clouded over as they were exploring the village that had been engulfed by deadly volcanic ash and debris one night in 1886, when the nearby mountain, Tarawera, erupted in a terrifying explosion that blew its conical top right off and irrevocably altered the landscape for miles about. The famous pink and white terraces had been lost in the upheaval, and existed now only in old sepia photographs and often garish nineteenth-century paintings. And the pathetic remnants of the dwellings that had once been a flourishing village had been dug out of the ashes to make a tourist attraction, the pots and dishes and trappings of everyday living placed about them. There were notices retelling the stories of people who had experienced the terror of the night of fire, when one hundred and fifty three people died, and the hut of one who had been trapped for days and miraculously recovered alive was signposted.

Sebastian examined it all with interest, and Roxanne with fascinated horror. Afterwards they moved on to Waimangu, for a walk through some of the thermal 'wonders' that had been left in the wake of the eruption—milk-white silica terraces perpetually washed with a thin film of water, bubbling mud holes, and a deep-set, supposedly bottomless lake of boiling water lying at the foot of steaming cliffs encrusted with the ever-present yellow sulphur.

They had a late lunch at a tea-rooms overlooking the restless, steaming valley, and then the rain came down and they returned to the city, visited the little Maori centre at Ohinemutu with its statue of Queen

Victoria atop a carved column in Maori design, and admired the church there. Inside, the intricate traditional weaving and carving were complemented by a huge modern window on which was sandblasted the figure of Christ in a feathered cloak, superimposed on the view of the lake, so that he appeared to be walking on water.

Here, the tension that had gripped Roxanne began to ease a little, her interest in the craftsmanship which had gone into the decoration of the church taking over, as she inspected the carvings and woven flax wall coverings.

When they emerged, the rain was pouring down, and they had to make a dash back to the car.

Watching the water washing down the windscreen, Sebastian said, 'We may as well make for the hotel, I suppose. We could collect some swimming gear and go to the Blue Baths.'

Swimming in warm mineral water was a prospect that appealed, in this weather, and she agreed eagerly. He looked at her thoughtfully, and started the car.

Some time later, as she floated lazily in the blue water of the pool, watching Sebastian take a high dive from the board, she found tears mingling with the droplets of water on her cheeks. A honeymoon should mean almost perfect happiness, a time for a man and woman who loved each other to learn about so many things, to share so many intimate secrets. What sort of honeymoon were they going to have, with Sebastian claiming rights without love, and herself determined not to give them, wary of his every move, every moment of softness?

She closed her eyes, trying to blot out thought, blot out feeling, make her mind blank for a time. The warmth of the water, the slow steam rising from it, were soporific, and she had almost succeeded in her aim when hard fingers brushed her damp cheek and

Sebastian's voice said, 'Hey, are you asleep?'

'I was, nearly,' she said, opening her eyes.

'Don't. You could drown that way.'

'Maybe that wouldn't be a bad idea,' she said flippantly,

It was obviously no joke to Sebastian. His eyes sparkling dangerously, he said, 'Don't be a little fool! If you're unhappy, it's your own fault. You're too scared to reach out and grab what's within your reach.'

'Maybe I don't want what's within my reach,' she retorted. 'Maybe I want something that you've effectively put out of my reach!'

She turned over in the water to swim away from him, but he grabbed her arm and stopped her.

'Like what?' he asked gratingly. 'You told me you didn't want Mark.'

'Like freedom!' she said. 'I suppose you can't conceive that I might not want a man at all?'

He grinned. 'You're not the cold little fish you like to make out you are, Roxanne. I've seen the ice melt once or twice. And it'll melt again—for me.'

Derisively, she said, 'What makes you think you're so irresistible? I was *acting*, that night on the beach, remember?'

A group of young boys erupted into the pool, yelling and splashing, and she took advantage of the diversion to wrench free of him and swim to the side, where she hauled herself out. She had been in long enough, anyway, the water was enervating after half an hour or so. She sat at the side for a while, watching the others swimmers, returned for a brief dip herself, then went off to get changed.

After dinner they sat in one of the lounges, and while Sebastian was in conversation with another guest, Roxanne murmured an excuse and slipped away to their room. She showered and got into bed, opening a paperback she had brought with her, but the strain of the day, the swim in the hot pool, and the dinner combined to make her genuinely sleepy. Long before Sebastian came into the room she was asleep with the book fallen to the covers beside her.

They spent the following day at one of the trout springs, wandering along bush-lined paths and watching the lazy spotted and rainbow fish swimming in deep water so pellucid that every tiny pebble on the stream bed was clearly visible. The weather had improved, and Sebastian bought them a picnic lunch which they ate on a grassy bank near a stream, the underwater springs that fed it making champagne bubbles as they forced their way through the earth's crust. Lying back on his hands in the shade of a lace-fronded ponga, Sebastian said, 'There's a carving and weaving school at Whaka—shall we go and see it, later?'

'If you like.' She was making a business of stuffing the paper wrappings from their lunch into a bundle, and feeding the crumbs to inquisitive sparrows and pigeons, and one or two bold fantails who had gathered about.

'A friend told me that the most likely time to see Pohutu perform is late afternoon.'

Roxanne didn't particularly want to see the geyser perform. She had vivid memories of it from her childhood visit to Rotorua, and felt that once in a lifetime was enough. But she didn't want Sebastian to know about her silly little phobias. Without comment, she went on feeding the birds until there were no more crumbs left. Then she got up to deposit the rubbish in a receptacle provided several yards away.

When she came back, Sebastian had his eyes closed and had apparently gone to sleep. She stood for a few moments looking down at him, his dark, narrow face relaxed now, without losing any of its strength of character. His mouth in repose looked less ruthless but still firm, and she was surprised and shocked by a sudden desire to put her lips to his and kiss him into awareness of her.

She sat down a few feet away from him, her back against the harsh bark of a totara, and closed her own eyes. Depression settled on her soul. Sebastian had barely touched her at all today, but she knew it couldn't last. He had told her he wasn't a patient man, although she was sure he could exercise considerable self-restraint if he thought that eventually it would get him what he wanted. She was certain he had not given up, but was merely biding his time. From his point of view, he couldn't lose. They were legally married, they were together, he wanted her and he must know that she didn't find him totally unattractive. It was inevitable that sooner or later nature and proximity would lead to an irresistible conclusion.

So why couldn't she just accept it? Why go on with this futile resistance, making him angry and more bitter?

And the answer came into her mind, *Because I want it to be a loving thing, not the payment of a debt, not the exacting of the terms of a coldblooded contract.*

And surely he had loved her, once? A man didn't propose marriage without loving, did he—? not a man like Sebastian. And, her mind suddenly as clear as the crystal springs that fed the stream flowing a few feet away, Roxanne told herself, *No, he wouldn't.* And she realised that, loving her, he must have been dealt a savage blow when she told him why she had pretended to agree to marry him.

At the time, she admitted to herself, she had deliberately blanked out of her mind any consideration of Sebastian's feelings. Only her father and her family, her love and concern for them, had been allowed to influence her actions. It had been, really, a monstrous thing to do.

And now wasn't she still bent on cheating him? she accused herself with shame. How long could she expect him to go on being patient, in the face of her hostility and her unwillingness to honour the terms of their bargain?

And there it was again, the thing that she could not accept. Perhaps Sebastian had been deeply hurt, and that was the basis of his determination to make her follow through on her empty promise to him. Or perhaps he had been so disillusioned when he discovered her motives that he no longer felt any love for her, only the need to revenge himself for being made a fool of.

Surely it was unbelievable that any man would go as far as marriage, for such a reason? She tried to tell herself it wasn't possible, that it must have been an excuse because he loved her and couldn't let her go. But her growing knowledge of him would not allow that comfort.

Wanting was not the same as loving, and there had been nothing loving in his treatment of her before the wedding, after he had found out her deception. If he had seemed to soften slightly since, it was only two days, after all. And even a man who intended to take a woman out of revenge might prefer a willing, eager partner rather than a frightened, frigid one.

No, she couldn't count on Sebastian's love. And with the deliberate, harsh admission to herself that she might have lost that for ever came the tearing, unexpected pain of knowing that she wanted it above everything in life, and why . . .

She was still reeling from the shock of discovering her own feelings when, later in the afternoon, they watched the master carver instructing his apprentices at the carving school. She scarcely listened to the explanation of how the old arts had appeared to be dying out, until a resurgence in interest had led to the setting up of the village and the school, with the aim of educating not only new craftsmen, but also their fellow New Zealanders and the tourists who came to watch and admire.

They walked down into the thermal area afterwards, Sebastian holding aloof from her, and Roxanne trying desperately to conceal her growing need for some kind of reassurance. As they descended, skirting fenced pools of boiling grey mud, and sulphurous holes from which eddied jets of steaming water, she began to feel again the overwhelming terror which as a child the place had engendered in her. It had seemed to her then that this was what was meant when they sang the psalm in church about walking 'in the valley of the shadow of death'. Not long before the Challis family visited Rotorua, a woman had either accidentally or deliberately slipped into one of the many boiling pools of water, and died. Roxanne had heard it reported on the television news, and as she held her father's hand tightly, religiously keeping her small feet on the narrow pumice paths between the sinister 'attractions' of hot mud and water, her childish imagination had been working feverishly. She was revolted by the overwhelming smell of sulphur, and by the sullen bubbling of the mud, often surrounded by sticks and decayed bits of vegetation and sometimes soft drink bottles and cans which some visitors had thrown into them, curious to see what would happen. In one evil-looking dark pond like a giant porridge pot on the boil, the half-decayed, atrophied body of some small animal, a cat or an opossum, lay skeletally pathetic and somehow horrible, near the edge, its hind legs on the heaving mud, so that with each slimy upheaval it twitched grotesquely.

They had seemed to stand there for a long time, while she watched in unwilling fascination, before her father tugged her hand and they went on down the path.

Now Sebastian was with her, but he didn't hold her hand, although now and then he placed light fingers on her elbow when the path was steep and narrow. He seemed interested and anxious to view all the phenomena of the volcanic activity about them, and by the time they had reached the area about Pohutu, past the pretty little 'Bridal Veil' falls, she was smouldering with a quite unjustified resentment born of a fear which she had done her utmost to hide, and of the knowledge that he had no idea of her feelings—either her fear or her newly discovered love.

A party of tourists were standing about, listening intently to their Maori guide, dressed in the traditional costume, a red bodice and flax skirt dramatically patterned in black, with a woven headband. Pohutu was issuing forth jets of steam and occasional gushes of hot water, spilling over on to the smooth white rock, and Sebastian wandered about, trying for a good vantage point if it should decide to play in earnest. He held out his hand to her, as he went closer, but Roxanne shook her head, her mouth tight, and he raised his eyebrows, shrugged, and turned away.

Then the ground beneath her feet began to vibrate, and a deep, ominous roaring came from under the earth.

'Sebastian! Be careful!' she cried.

He turned and gave her a surprised, quizzical grin as she took an involuntary step towards him. 'It's okay,' he assured her. 'I won't get too close for safety.' There were little notices pegged into the ground defining the safe margin, and he stopped with his feet almost touching one of them.

Then the geyser hurled itself up in front of them, a long, powerful column of boiling hot water, roaring like a beast out of control. The tourists exclaimed and applauded, and raised their cameras to capture the impressive sight, and Roxanne saw Sebastian's head go up, a grin of pleasure on his face as he tried to view the top of the geyser.

Well, he was getting a splendid view, she thought bitterly, as she backed away, swallowing down her irrational, childish fear. Eddies of steam floated across the area, blocking out the view of the hillside, and then the wind changed, and Sebastian disappeared in a white cloud of steam, that then engulfed her, warm and choking. She felt droplets of spray on her face and turned instinctively, stumbling as she tried to escape the warm, wet cloud. Her fear became panic, and she put a hand up, trying vainly to push way the steam that blinded her, and began to run.

The hard white silica gave way to sulphur-encrusted earth, and she felt her foot plunge into a hole, a hole where sudden heat jetted against her ankle. She fell and scraped her hands on rough stones, jerking her foot away with horror, her mind filled by nightmare visions of a hidden, scalding pool into which she was about to drop, of the thin crust of earth giving way and allowing her to be sucked down into the hell that boiled and bubbled below. She cried out in terror.

She heard Sebastian calling her name, and then close by there was a soft, clacking sound and a blur of red. A brown hand touched her arm, and as she realised it was the Maori guide, in her flax *piu-piu* and red underskirt, Sebastian emerged from the steam and helped the woman pull her to her feet.

She clutched at him as the steam thinned and floated away from them. His arms felt strong and solid, and he demanded sharply, 'What happened? Are you all right?'

She realised that she was, and took a hold of herself, easing away from him, and clamping her teeth tightly on the hysteria that had momentarily overcome her. 'I put my foot in a hole,' she said, annoyed to find that her voice was shaking. 'It scared me for a moment.'

She hadn't been scalded, the hole was just a small depression in the earth, and although there was steam issuing from it, the trickle of water that ran on to the yellow earth was only of hot-bath temperature. 'It was the steam,' she explained. 'I couldn't see.'

The guide was looking at her with shrewd brown eyes. 'It's better to keep still round here, if you can't see where you're going,' she said, with a hint of sternness.

'Yes,' Roxanne said. 'I'm sorry. Thank you for coming to rescue me.'

The woman smiled and patted her arm. 'That's all right. Gave yourself a fright, didn't you? You look pretty pale, even for a Pakeha.'

Roxanne returned a shaky smile of her own, and the guide said to Sebastian, 'She looks like she could do with a drink. You'd better get her one, eh?'

'A very good idea,' Sebastian agreed, as the woman returned to her tourist party. 'Let's go.'

'Are you sure you've seen enough?' Roxanne enquired, with a hint of weary sarcasm.

Sebastian glanced at her sharply, a frown in his eyes. 'Yes,' he said, and firmly took her arm. 'And I'm damned sure that *you* have.'

Back at the hotel, he steered her into one of the lounges and ordered drinks. Two strong gin-and-tonics later, she found the room wasn't quite still when she stood up, and realised that it was several hours since lunch, and that she was quite unused to alcohol on an empty stomach.

She managed to make it to their room, and once there was very glad to slip off her shoes and lie at full length on her bed. Sebastian sat on the side of it, his arm across her as his hand rested on the bed, at the other side of her body.

'All right now?' he queried.

'Yes. I'll just rest a while, and then change before we eat.'

'You weren't joking when you said you hated this place, were you?' he said. 'Why on earth did you suggest it?'

She looked away. 'I was being facetious—you know that. The place all the loving couples go to for their honeymoon.'

He was quiet, sitting perfectly still. Then he got up and went into the bathroom, and Roxanne shut her eyes and pretended to be dozing.

Sebastian scarcely spoke to her over their dinner, and his unusual taciturnity made her nervous. She drank a lot of wine, and began to feel lightheaded and rather daring. The band was playing again, and when they had finished their coffee, she said, 'Let's dance.'

The look he gave her was cool and assessing, but he said, 'All right—if that's what you want.'

On the small dance floor she melted into his arms, her face against his jacket, eyes closed. She wanted to be near him, to feel him holding her. He held her tightly, and it was blissful. It no longer mattered whether he loved her or despised her. She loved him, and wanted him, and that would be enough for them both, for now. When he feathered his lips along her brow, she raised her face to his and felt his lips touch hers briefly before he said abruptly, 'Let's go up.'

They took the lift, and its cool interior seemed to chill her a little, that and the fact that Sebastian had removed his supporting arm as he pressed the button to take them up to their floor. He put a light hand on her waist to guide her along the carpeted corridor, and when the door of their room closed behind them he switched on the central light, making her blink in its glare.

Roxanne walked over to the window and drew the curtains, slipping out of her shoes as she did so. Then she turned to smile at him, and found him standing just inside the door, very still, his face dark and harsh-looking.

'Sebastian?' she queried, disturbed and anxious.

He took a step, two steps towards her, and she held out a hand, inviting, pleading.

He came closer and took her hand, jerking her forward into his arms, kissing her with hunger and violence, tipping back her head into his hand, making her open her mouth and sliding down his other hand to grind her body against his. A shudder of fear and pleasure ran through her, and she clutched wildly at him, at first simply to keep her balance, and then in a frenzy of passionate response.

He stopped kissing her mouth, and his lips scorched her throat, before he swung her off her feet and put her down on the bed.

Her hands went up about his neck to pull him down with her, but he was sitting on the bed, his arms on each side of her, and resisted her embrace.

Roughly he said, 'Do you want me to come to bed with you, Roxanne? Do you want to make love?'

Her hands caressing his shoulders, she nodded, shyly. 'Please, Sebastian.' She linked her fingers again behind his neck, and looked into his eyes, her eyes bright with love and need. 'Darling——'

Instead of coming down to join her on the bed, he jerked her suddenly into a sitting position, her head bent back over his arm as he kissed her again, his mouth moving over hers savagely, until she whimpered with the bruising force of it.

When he stopped at last, and removed his arms, she fell back against the pillow white-faced and gasping.

He said, 'You've had a bad fright, and you're more than a little sloshed. And I don't think I care to accept your—invitation, under those circumstances. I want you very aware and in your right mind, and *wanting me*. Right now, all you want is some sort of comfort. Well, I'm not your teddy bear—nor your father. Ask me again when you're back to your cool, competent self—and sober. Then I might be interested.'

Watching him walk away from her, hauling off his jacket and pulling open the buttons on his shirt as he undressed, Roxanne thought she couldn't have been more sober than at this moment. His rejection had shocked her out of her rosy, alcoholic haze and into sharp, cold sanity. But now was not the time to say so, to renew her invitation. Rather obviously, he wasn't in the mood.

Stripped to his underpants, he went into the bathroom, and Roxanne turned over on her side, facing away from his bed, so that when he returned she could pretend to be asleep. He wasn't going to make it easy for her, and in all honesty she couldn't really see why he should. Only she wasn't sure that, after that brutal refusal, she would ever be capable of renewing her offer in a state of stone-cold sobriety.

CHAPTER EIGHT

In the morning, Sebastian wasn't there when Roxanne woke. She had dressed and was pinning up her hair when he came into the room, looking vital and darkly handsome in an open cream shirt and tan slacks. His hair was slightly less tidy than usual, and he seemed to bring with him a tang of the open air.

'Where have you been?' she asked him.

'Missed me?' He didn't wait for an answer to his sardonic question, but said, 'Out walking. Would you like to go back home?'

She swung round from the mirror, the comb in her hand forgotten. Sebastian met her startled eyes with a grim smile. 'To my house,' he said. 'At the beach. *Our* new home, remember?'

He had evidently been thinking as he walked, deciding that their honeymoon was a dead loss, probably. Roxanne thought about the house by the beach, secluded and peaceful, the air fresh and sweet with the scents of bush and sea. 'Yes,' she said. 'Yes, I would—please.'

They spent the morning shopping and left after lunch, Roxanne feeling much less tense than she had over the past three days, and Sebastian silent and remote looking and intent on his driving.

After a long while, she said, 'I'm sorry I was so stupid yesterday—at Whaka.'

'Stupid?'

She chewed briefly on her lower lip. 'I was scared,' she confessed. 'The place made me nervous as a child, and I'm afraid I've never grown out of it. I don't expect you to understand——'

'Why not?'

Roxanne shrugged. She couldn't imagine Sebastian suffering from childish fears.

As though he had read her mind, he said, 'If you want to see me scream and run, shut me in a confined space with a wasp. I got stung on the eyelid when I was a kid, and I've never forgotten it. Apart from the pain, I thought I was blinded.'

He was smiling slightly, but it wasn't funny. Of course he wouldn't scream and run, but he might well sweat a bit, with childhood memories goading him. Roxanne wondered what sort of little boy he had been—a lonely one, she guessed, from the little he had let slip about his family life.

The trip was long, and Sebastian took a back road round the outskirts of Waimiro which made it rather longer, but reduced the chances of anyone in the town knowing of their return. Roxanne was thankful for that. She didn't want to have to provide excuses to the curious for cutting their honeymoon short.

A pale sunset washed the sky with faint pinks and golds as Sebastian pushed open the door of the house, and unexpectedly swept her up into his arms and stepped inside. 'Might as well do the thing properly,' he said, but his kiss was brief, over before she had realised what was happening. He put her down and said, 'Switch on some lights, will you? I'll get the bags.'

She turned on lights in the passage and kitchen, and was making coffee when he came in. She paused with a spoonful of instant coffee poised over a cup as she heard him go into the main bedroom with the cases. He came out again and headed straight for the kitchen, and she knew that he had not entered the smaller room with its single bed.

She spooned the coffee into the cup, and when he came in didn't look up, but her fingers were unsteady as she picked up the sugar bowl and put it on the small table.

'Do you want something to eat?' she asked.

'I can wait. I left some eggs, and there's the groceries we bought this morning. Do you want to cook, or shall I?'

'I'll do it.' She poured hot water on to the coffee and placed the cups on the table.

They sat opposite each other, sipping the hot fluid, Roxanne's eyes fixed on the cup.

'What's the matter?' Sebastian asked.

Forcing herself to look up, she said, 'Nothing.'

He looked at her measuringly, then drained his cup and stood up. 'I'll unpack my things. There's plenty of room for yours, by the way. Six drawers and more than half the wardrobe to yourself.'

His eyes mocked her, and she said, 'Thank you. I'll get unpacked later.'

They had bought a few vegetables, meat and milk, tacitly acknowledging that they didn't want to have to go into Waimiro for stores. Roxanne made a cole-slaw, liberally laced with dry mustard and ground black pepper so that it smelled spicily appetising; grilled two slices of steak and a couple of halved tomatoes, then placed golden-yolked fried eggs on top. She set the small kitchen table rather than the round mahogany one in the dining corner of the lounge, and called Sebastian.

It was quite dark outside now, the kitchen light bright and almost harsh by contrast. Sebastian glanced at the table, then at Roxanne's face, and took long-stemmed glasses and a bottle of red wine from one of the cupboards.

When he placed the filled glass in front of her as she sat down, she said, 'Thank you.'

'Shouldn't we have candles?'

'I expect you'd rather be able to see what you're

eating—and I don't suppose you have any candles, anyway.'

'Then you suppose wrong.'

He went to a drawer, fished in a cupboard, and produced two long creamy wax candles, pushed into a matching pair of simple but well made pottery candle holders. A match scraped and he put the candles on the table, slightly to each side, then switched off the light.

Immediately the table assumed an intimate atmosphere, and as he sat down, Roxanne tried to dispel it, saying in a brittle voice, 'I had no idea you were such a romantic, Sebastian.'

'Didn't you?' he said with cold deliberation. 'You seem to harbour a great many misconceptions about me.'

She looked at him warily. In the soft, flickering light, he looked amused but somehow strangely menacing. Nervously she picked up her knife and fork and began to eat.

'You haven't touched your wine,' Sebastian reminded her, when she had almost finished her steak.

She sipped at it and put the glass down. 'It's good,' she said. 'But a bit dry for my taste.'

'There's some white if you'd prefer it.'

Roxanne shook her head. 'Do you want a dessert? There's ice cream and tinned fruit.'

'No. This will do.' He reached for an apple from a bowl she had placed on the table, alongside a dish of cheddar. 'Want some?'

'A half,' she said, pushing aside her plate.

Sebastian deftly halved the apple and quartered it, removing the core with the knife before placing two neat quarters on her side plate.

The crisp fruit was sweet and refreshing, and a slice of bland cheese to follow made a pleasant ending to the meal. She took another sip of her wine, while

Sebastian was pouring himself a second glass. 'Coffee?' she asked him.

'No, thanks, not for me.'

'Then I won't bother, either.'

Roxanne took the empty plates and put them in the sink, then cleared the few things from the table while Sebastian sat finishing the wine in his glass. He refilled it again from the bottle, and stood up. 'I'll pour you some white,' he said, 'and we can sit in the other room.'

'No, thanks. I want to stay sober.'

There was an electric silence, and she knew he was willing her to look at him. At last he drawled, 'Now, that could mean a number of interesting things.'

'All it means is what I said,' she assured him huskily. 'I had more than enough to drink last night.'

'What are you regretting?' he asked. 'Your—interesting reaction, or the fact that I declined your generous offer?'

Averting her eyes as she walked past him into the lounge, she said, 'Perhaps I'm regretting the headache I had this morning.'

On a breath of reluctant laughter, he said, 'Perhaps.' He blew out the candles and followed her, turning on a table lamp, but leaving most of the lounge shadowed as he took her arm and firmly pushed her on to the long sofa, seating himself beside her.

He still held his glass, and although she sat stiffly, he seemed relaxed as he slid an arm along the back of the sofa behind her. Outside the window the moon was a huge orb of orange, hanging just over the dimly seen tips of the trees. The sea was black and inky, and far-flung stars against the night defined the sky. A huge green puriri moth fluttered against the window for several seconds, then disappeared into the night, and some of its smaller relatives crawled persistently over the glass, narrow wings folded, or waving briefly as they slithered down the smooth surface, only to renew their effort to find an entry to the hypnotic light within.

Sebastian said, 'Would you like some music?'

Roxanne shook her head. The distant pounding of the waves on the unseen sand was music enough. 'I should unpack,' she said.

'Don't move.' Sebastian stopped her tentative movement with a hand on her shoulder, pulling her back against him, so that her soft hair was against his cheek and jaw. 'You can unpack later. Relax, now.'

He continued to sip at his wine, and after a few moments she let the tension seep from her and obeyed him, her eyes half closed as his thumb moved gently over the silk of her sleeve, sensitising the skin beneath the loose blouse. She felt his lips touch her temple, then he put down the empty wine glass on the floor beside him, and his fingers came under her chin, making her look at him.

His eyes were dark and demanding, and as they slid to her mouth she felt sudden heat lick over her skin.

'You look half asleep,' he said critically.

'It's been a tiring day.'

He bent his head and kissed her, long and hard, his fingers sliding to her neck and then up again to hold her face up to him, almost hurting as they probed her skin.

Roxanne closed her eyes against the onslaught, and when his mouth lifted her lashes fluttered up only a little. Still holding her, Sebastian said, 'Too tired to fight me?'

Her eyes opened then, slowly, staring at him. 'Do you want me to fight you?'

'No, I want you to respond to me, damn you!'

His voice was soft, but frustration was darkening his eyes and making his jawline tight.

Roxanne smiled faintly, pleased at the small revenge for last night. And Sebastian's eyes narrowed, glinting dangerously, as he saw the challenge and the rejection in hers.

His eyes still holding hers, he began to tug open the buttons on her blouse, one by one. He separated the edges and pushed them back before his gaze lowered to take in the lightly tanned skin and the swell of her breasts beneath a white lace bra that dipped in the front to a single hook fastening. One hand slid on to the skin of her back, and the forefinger of the other touched her lips lightly, went briefly to test the small, beating pulse in the hollow of her throat, and slid straight down to the little valley between her breasts.

For a long moment she held her breath, waiting for him to part the fastening. Instead, his finger wandered again, following the scalloped edge of the bra over the curve of her breast, sending tiny thrills of pleasure racing along her nerves as it returned to the shadowed, shallow cleft, and did the same along the edge of the other cup.

Roxanne drew a shuddering breath. 'Sebastian . . .'

'Yes?' His voice was soft, his finger resting just above the clasp again.

She looked into his eyes, dark, unfathomable, trying to see the answer to the question she dared not ask. She saw only leashed desire and amused speculation. Closing her own eyes defeatedly, she said, 'Nothing.' Her head turned away from his scrutiny, and her body sagged against his arm. All at once she felt deathly tired.

For long moments Sebastian didn't move. Then he shifted her to sit with her back against the sofa, and began doing up her blouse. She opened surprised eyes as he hauled her to her feet. 'Come on,' he said. 'We're going for a walk on the beach. *Something's* got to wake you up.'

'It's dark!' she protested. 'I don't want to go beach walking at this time of night.'

'I know the path like the back of my hand,' he told her. 'And there's a full moon.'

He opened the door to the terrace and made her walk beside him, his hand gripping her upper arm.

The trees set up a muted rustling as a sea-borne breeze stirred their leaves, and a lone insect added its solo chirp to the booming of the waves, the hushed music of the bush, and the distant intermittent calling of a marauding night bird. The sand when they reached it was cool and white in the moonlight, and the wind blew an occasional fine mist of spray along the edge of the waves, the white spuming crests moving restlessly against the blackly gleaming sea.

Spray touched Roxanne's face, and she licked its salt taste from her lips. The sand under her feet yielded softly, and the breeze seemed to blow right into her mind, sweeping away the confusion and doubt and bringing her into a confrontation with her own feelings.

The wind sharpened, and she shivered in its cool caress. Sebastian asked, 'Are you cold?' and shifted his arm to lie over her shoulders. But she said, 'No,' breaking away from him to kick off her shoes and wade into the darkened sea. A wave rushed out of the night, and she held her skirt, bunching it in her hands above her knees, feeling the tug of the undertow, the stinging cold of the salt water against her bare legs, and the sand beneath her feet eroding away with the receding water.

She knew Sebastian was watching her, and after a while she heard him say, as a bigger wave rushed in and over her thighs, catching the edges of her skirt even as she held it, 'Are you going to swim?'

He sounded amused, not really meaning it. It was too cold to swim, but she felt reckless and uninhibited.

She turned and waded out of the water, running a few yards along the beach away from him. Then she pulled down the zip of her skirt and let it fall to the sand while she doffed the thin blouse and dropped that, too.

Sebastian stood quite still, watching her, and when she had finished she ran back into the water without looking at him. When he joined her, his bare shoulders gleaming in the moonlight, she felt a surge of triumph, but turned to swim away from him, her heart hammering.

The flimsy briefs and bra she wore were no more substantial than a bikini. But when Sebastian caught her and pulled her against the length of his body in the water, she experienced a thrill of shock as she realised that he had gone one better, and was swimming totally nude. She threshed wildly against his imprisoning hands, and as they slipped along her limbs, managed to dive away from him, coming up at the crest of an incoming breaker and laughing as it crashed down on Sebastian's black head.

She was still laughing when his hard fingers closed about her ankle, and she managed to gulp in a breath before he pulled her under and then let her go, to find him waiting for her on the surface, a white grin on his face as he grabbed her hair and pressed a brief, salty kiss on her lips before she pushed her fingers into his wet hair and ducked him in turn. He took her with him, and they separated and surfaced gasping and laughing into the air, to find another breaker descending on them.

They rode it in to the beach together, and emerged from the water shivering with cold. Sebastian pulled on his pants and Roxanne found her blouse and pushed her wet arms into it. She couldn't find her shoes, and her skirt was wet in great patches, so she rolled it up and took Sebastian's hand as he slung his shirt over one shoulder and began walking quickly towards the path.

She was panting when they reached the top, the nippy breeze raising goose pimples on her bare legs. As he pushed her inside the house, she put her arms about herself and tried to stop shivering.

'You little idiot!' he snapped, as he turned from shutting the door. 'You're freezing.'

She grinned at him and said, 'Well, I'm wide awake.'

Narrow-eyed, he surveyed her, the silk shirt clinging wetly to the soaked underthings and skin beneath it. Roxanne looked right back, her eyes smiling an invitation and a challenge.

'Into the bathroom,' he said abruptly. 'Towels.'

He followed her, pulled a big towel out of a cupboard and handed it to her while he quickly found another and rubbed it over his hair and face.

Roxanne dried her face, then stood reflectively rubbing at her hair while she watched the play of muscle in his arms and torso appreciatively.

Sebastian threw the towel he was using down on a stool, and she stopped looking, turning away slightly as she industriously dried her hair. The blouse had absorbed most of the water from her body, and her legs had dried on the way up, in the breeze, but damp tendrils of hair were still sending rivulets of water over her shoulders.

Sebastian said, 'You'd better get out of that wet blouse.'

'I'll have to unpack something else to wear,' she said practically.

'Will you?'

She looked at him quickly, noting the peculiar tone in which he said it, and what she saw in his eyes brought a flush of colour to her cheeks.

He came over to her, and her hands stilled on the towel as for the second time that evening he pushed back the edges of her blouse. This time he didn't stop there, but slipped it from her shoulders and let it lie on the floor. He took the towel from her unresisting fingers and draped it about her shoulders, letting the wet hair fall over it.

'So, you're awake,' he said.

'Yes.'

'And aware.'

'Yes,' she said, unafraid.

His finger began again on the path he had traced earlier, moving along the edge of the damp white bra. 'And sober?' he queried softly.

'Oh, very. I've hardly touched a drop all night.'

His eyes left hers to follow the movement of his finger, teasing at the clip, pulling a little to bring her closer, but not unfastening the hook. Then he slid his finger and thumb into the lace cup, and closed them over her nipple. Roxanne gasped with sudden incredible pleasure, and he laughed, brief and low, and brought his hand up to raise her face to his gaze. 'And wanting me!' he said with soft triumph. His other hand was on the small of her back, hauling her closer to him, his mouth inches from her parted lips.

She whispered his name, pleadingly, and he swung her into his arms and carried her into the bedroom. He placed her on the black silk spread, and asked, 'Are you still cold?'

She shook her head, but she was shivering, with excitement and a residue of fear.

The towel had fallen from her shoulders as he carried her, and he lifted her, pulled the bedspread away and let her damp tangled hair spread over the clean pillow. His hands slid over her limbs, and he leaned over to pull the sheet and blanket down at the other side of her. 'Move over,' he ordered, 'and get in.'

Obediently, she slipped under the covers, and watched shyly as the moonlight pouring in the big window outlined his naked body when he swiftly shed what little clothing he had been wearing.

He came into the bed beside her and his hands found and explored the cool skin of her shoulders, waist and thighs. His fingers unerringly discovered the hook of her bra and pulled it apart, and waves of heat suffused her body as his hands and his mouth caressed her in ways she had scarcely dreamed of. By the time his hand tugged at the band of her panties, she was eager to help him remove that last, modest barrier. Her shaking fingers stroked his back and shoulders, and when he said hoarsely, 'Now, darling!' she held him to her and let him part her legs with his, without fear.

It was strange, but he was gentle, although she felt the tenseness that was in him as he controlled the uncontrollable, for her sake.

'Am I hurting you!' he whispered, his mouth against her cheek. And she said, 'No.' It was a lie, but not much of a lie, because the pain was nothing compared to the pleasure that was increasing with every second, and although once she had nearly cried out, the pang had quickly receded.

Sebastian touched her mouth with his, and she felt the slight trembling of his lips, and opened her own to him, warm and passionately loving. He kissed her deeply, and she felt the trembling spread throughout his body, and arched against him in triumph and anticipation.

He wrenched his mouth from hers and groaned, 'Oh God, *no*! I want you to feel it too!'

'I do,' she gasped. 'I do—oh, don't stop! Please don't stop . . .'

Then sensation overwhelmed her, as she knew it was overwhelming him, and there were no more words until the storm of pleasure passed, and they lay quietly side by side, with her head against his shoulder, and his hand reflectively stroking her waist and hip.

'All right?' he asked her softly, his lips grazing her temple.

'Very much all right,' she said drowsily. 'Thank you, Sebastian.'

'Thank *you*,' he said gravely. 'My dear love.'

She thought that was what he said, but even as his murmured voice reached her ear, she was falling into a chasm of sleep that seemed deep enough to swallow her for ever, and the next day, she wondered if she had heard it at all.

In the morning she woke to the sound of rain drumming on the roof, and opened her eyes to find Sebastian leaning on one elbow, watching her.

'Good morning,' he said.

Realising that the covers had slipped during the night, Roxanne pulled up the sheet to cover her breasts. Sebastian grinned and slipped his hand over her, under the sheet, watching the wild colour in her cheeks with satisfaction.

'We'd better get up,' she said.

'What for? We're on our honeymoon, aren't we?'

'Sebastian, we can't stay in bed all day!'

He laughed. 'You want a bet?'

She resisted his effort to pull her closer to him, pushing against his bare chest and shaking her head. 'I want to go to the bathroom,' she said.

'Okay.' He lay back, his head on linked hands. 'Away you go, then.'

She sat up, the sheet clutched before her, and looked about the room. Her unopened case stood against the wall near the door. Her bra lay on the floor by the bed, and she couldn't see her panties. 'Sebastian,' she said, 'I've got nothing to put on.'

'There's only you and me here, honey.' He was watching her, in his eyes a wicked amusement. He ran a finger down her spine, and asked, 'What's the trouble?'

She turned her head to look at him, and said levelly, 'I think you know.'

Perhaps it was silly, in the circumstances, but it was more than she could do to walk across the room in broad daylight without a stitch on, with him watching.

He sat up, tilted her chin and kissed her, his unshaven skin grazing hers. Then he slid out of the bed, went to the wardrobe and shrugged into a knee-length robe, tying the belt quickly before picking up her case and heaving it on to the bed.

'There you are,' he said. 'I'll have a quick shower and shave while you find what you want.'

When he came back ten minutes later, she was wearing the pink robe.

He said, 'It's all yours,' and she picked up her toilet things and went along to the bathroom.

Her hair was tangled, and she washed it under the shower and used conditioner, combed it out while it was wet, and put a clean towel about her shoulders over the robe before returning to the bedroom.

Sebastian wasn't there, but the smell of frying bacon wafting from the kitchen gave her a clue as to his whereabouts. She pulled a pair of jeans and a fine wool jersey from her case, and found some underclothes. She dressed quickly, unpacked her case, and made the bed. Sebastian appeared in the doorway as she was smoothing the cover over it. He was still in his bathrobe, and he looked critically at her practical clothing as he asked, 'Want some breakfast?'

'Thank you.' She turned to the dressing table and pinned her hair up before turning to join him. 'Aren't you getting dressed?'

'Does it bother you?'

She shook her head, and he said, 'After breakfast, then.'

The bacon was crisp and delicious, and he had fried tomatoes and eggs to go with it. He made coffee and, as she stirred sugar into hers, he said quietly, 'You're not regretting last night, are you, Roxanne?'

She shook her head and, daring to tease a little, looked up at him and said, 'Are you?'

'Are you kidding?' His eyes gave her the answer, and she smiled back at him as she put down the spoon and lifted the cup to her lips.

She finished first, and started clearing the table while he was still drinking his coffee. She had piled the breakfast things on top of the dishes from the night before, and was running hot water into the sink when he came behind her, placed his cup in the water and slid his hands about her waist, finding the smooth warm skin under the jersey.

Roxanne squeezed some detergent into the water, watching it foam, then turned off the taps. She said, 'I can't do this when you're holding me!' and tried to prise Sebastian's hands from her waist. He only tightened them and pulled her back against him, nuzzling at her neck with his lips. Roxanne sighed and relaxed, then her hands stopped pulling at his wrists and began to stroke his arms and his hands where they rested at her waist. His mouth touched her earlobe and gently bit it. 'Come back to bed, wife,' he murmured.

'The dishes——'

'Damn the dishes!' His hands moved over her skin to the band of her bra, and he released the hook and cupped her breasts in the warmth of his palms. Roxanne sighed and her own hands pressed his against her soft flesh. She felt the deep, shuddering breath that he took, his chest rising against her back. 'You're beautiful,' he muttered. 'No one else ever did this to you, did they?'

She shook her head, her eyes closed, as she savoured the slow, sweet excitement.

'I want to look at you,' he said, 'Come back to bed, honey. Let me see you . . .'

The dishes lay forgotten in the sink for a long time, the water cooled and the foam disappeared from its surface. The rain still hammered on the roof, but the two in the bedroom heard nothing, saw nothing, thought of nothing, but each other. For Roxanne, the world had narrowed to the circle of her husband's arms. Knowing that her body pleased him, that the scent of her still damp hair, the smooth texture of her skin, the softness of her breasts and the shape of her hips and legs, delighted him, she gradually became less shy of his almost greedy appraisal of her nakedness, and found an erotic pleasure of her own in allowing him to uncover it. The touch of his mouth was an intoxicant, and each kiss, each coming together was more satisfying than the last. She knew that he was taking great care to place her needs before his own, and it pleased her to reciprocate, to discover the ways she could use her hands and mouth and body to bring him to a peak of sensual joy equal to hers.

The days and nights that followed were magical, a short time stolen from eternity, while they discovered each other in a hundred ways, exchanged snatches of memories, intimate jokes, kisses and laughter and endearments. When the rain stopped and the sun glittered on the sea and sparkled on the wet leaves of the trees, they wandered along the beach with their arms about each other, and kissed while the wavelets rippled about their bare ankles. And when the sun was lost behind grey, scudding clouds and the trees danced frenziedly in a whistling wind, they stayed in the house and watched the wild breakers racing to shore, and made love on the sofa as the rain hurled against the windows and ran down the panes and pounded on the roof, drowning the incoherent, soft cries of their loving.

No one disturbed them, and they only wanted each other, but the day came when they would have been expected home, and Sebastian said, 'I'll have to go to Auckland tomorrow.'

'Yes,' Roxanne sighed. 'And I'm expected at the shop. It had to end some time.'

Sebastian looked at her and drew her close to him, and said, 'It won't end, Roxanne. This will never end.'

CHAPTER NINE

THE shop had survived very well in her absence. Her mother had offered to help Grace run it, and seemingly had enjoyed it so much she was almost reluctant to hand over again to Roxanne. With Rhonda away now at art school, and Roxanne married, she was finding she had time on her hands and only two to cook for.

'You and Sebastian must come to dinner,' she said eagerly. 'Tomorrow?'

'All right,' said Roxanne, 'provided Sebastian is free.'

The dinner was as usual superb, her mother sparkled and her father was jovial. When he was alone for a few moments with Roxanne, he said uncomfortably, 'You know, Roxanne, after the wedding I began to wonder if I'd fooled myself into thinking everything had turned out for the best. I was afraid you'd done something quixotic for the sake of the family, but I can see that I was wrong. You *are* happy, aren't you?'

'Happier than I ever expected,' she assured him. 'Perhaps happier than I deserve.'

'Oh, no, not that. I'm very glad for you, my dear. Very glad.'

On the way home, she said to Sebastian, 'We must ask them back, some time. Do you mind?'

'Of course not. There are some others we should invite as well.'

'A dinner party?'

'Would you like that? It's up to you.'

'It's a challenge. Who do you want to invite?'

'I owe Max Ansell some hospitality. And I saw Neal

yesterday. He and Felicia will be taking a week's holiday soon. They have a bach just up the coast that they use on odd weekends and holidays. If we could arrange it for that week, it might be convenient for them.'

'All right,' Roxanne said after a small silence. She liked Neal Osborne, but had never lost a sense of unease with his wife. At the wedding, Felicia had looked elegant in black, flowing and split to the hip, and she had kissed Roxanne's cheek with cool lips and slanted one of her enigmatic glances at Sebastian before doing the same to him, with the fingers of one hand touching his other cheek. Roxanne saw the colour rise in his skin under Felicia's painted fingertips, and the strange, almost tremulous smile she gave him as she drew away.

The memory surfaced now, disturbingly.

Ridiculous, she said to herself. Neal and Felicia were old friends of Sebastian's. Naturally he wanted to entertain them. The fact that Roxanne found it difficult to like or to relate to Felicia was neither here nor there. She didn't suppose that Sebastian was going to like all of her friends, either. There had to be some give and take, and she would make a special effort to get on with Felicia, in future.

'By the way,' she said, 'I'd like to ask Delia, if you don't mind.'

Sebastian grinned faintly. 'It might liven up the party, if Max decides to wring her neck, after all.'

'Max is a very civilised person.'

'No man is civilised when he's in love and angry about it.'

'It's time he stopped being angry. Delia's basically a very sweet girl.'

'That's the trouble. She's spread her sweetness about rather liberally, I gather.'

'Don't you like her?'

He looked sideways at her and said, 'Now, what

should I answer to that?'

Roxanne made a scornful, indignant little sound, and he grinned. 'Okay,' he said. 'I like her, but Max is welcome to her. Satisfied?'

'Maybe she doesn't want Max.'

'So why are you planning to throw them together?'

'Well, Max is certainly in love with her, and once he gets over being furious about her past, he'll probably make a good husband.'

'Were *you* ever interested in Max, Roxanne?' Sebastian asked.

'No. Not my type.'

'But Mark was?'

'Apparently not,' she said, wary of the silky note in his voice. 'I didn't marry Mark, did I?'

'No. But then I didn't give you much choice about marrying me, in the end.'

That was true, but she had no regrets, now. She wondered if he had. The silence was lengthening, becoming tense, and to lighten the moment, she said, 'Well, I decided to make the best of it, didn't I?'

Sebastian's foot hit the brake, bringing the car to a breath-jolting stop at the side of the road. He turned to her, his face taut. 'Is that what you're doing?' he demanded. 'Is that all it is with you?'

Her eyes wide and startled, she shook her head. 'I was joking,' she said shakily.

'Don't make jokes like that!' he muttered between his teeth, and his hands moulded her face between them as he bent his head to kiss her almost savagely.

He released her and started the engine again, his face grimly set. Roxanne touched her fingers to her stinging mouth and glanced at him with surprised speculation. He still wasn't sure of her, she realised. In spite of the passion, the loving that she had given him, he hadn't known that she loved him. Gazing at the windscreen oblivious to the view, she knew she had to tell him.

About to speak the words of reassurance, of love, she turned to him and was halted by the hardness of his profile, the cold expression in his eyes as he flicked an enquiring glance at her. With a sudden chill she realised that Sebastian, too, had been strangely reticent. He told her that she was beautiful, that he wanted her, that her body enchanted him, that he loved the taste of her mouth and the feel of her skin. He called her darling and made love to her with a concentrated passion and skill, but she couldn't think of any occasion when he had actually said, 'I love you.' Possibly she was reading something into this incident that wasn't there.

He wanted her to love him, that was certain. But she was suddenly unsure about his motives. The bubble of her unquestioning, mindless happiness was beginning to quiver, distorted by doubts, in danger of breaking.

The doubts remained with her in the days that followed, even though she tried to thrust them aside, and remind herself that when she had given herself wholeheartedly to her husband and her marriage, it was without reservation, without demanding that her love should be returned. She was haunted by the fear that Sebastian was awaiting her complete capitulation, that he still had some subtle, uncompleted plan of revenge. But when he made love to her, her ardent response to his touch swamped fear and distrust, convincing her that she was imagining bogeys where none existed. She told herself she was being absurd, and Sebastian's gentleness and passion erased her uncertainties.

The dinner guests were a mixed group. Roxanne's parents were older than most of the others, but having made the acquaintance of a middle-aged couple living in one of the three neighbouring houses, the only one permanently occupied rather than used only for holidays, Roxanne had invited them along. Grace Sherwood and her husband were delighted to accept an invitation, and Delia, after some persuasion from Roxanne, agreed to come, too. Roxanne had told her that Max was coming, but had decided not to let Max know that she intended inviting Delia.

Mr and Mrs Challis arrived first, and Max soon afterwards. The Sherwoods, bringing Delia with them, were late, and it was with some relief that Roxanne learned that their tardiness was due not to any last-minute flutterings of Delia's but to Grace's recalcitrant offspring, the youngest of whom had needed a great deal of reassurance from his mother before consenting to accept the babysitter.

Max was talking to Felicia Osborne when Delia swept in, her head, topped by a gleaming blonde coil of hair, held high, and a dramatically simple black velvet skirt and white satin blouse giving her an air of unmistakable elegance.

Heads turned, and Roxanne saw Felicia, wearing a low-cut red dress that emphasised her black hair and creamy skin, sweep her gaze over the newcomer with cold calculation. *She doesn't like competition*, Roxanne thought. *Good for you, Delia!*

Immediately she chided herself for being catty, and shifted her glance to Max. He looked remarkably wooden, but she fancied that the dark flush in his cheeks wasn't altogether due to the drinks he had consumed, which had not been many, nor to Felicia's figure, which he had been eyeing with appreciation but also with equanimity, for some time.

He nodded unsmilingly to Delia and turned back to Felicia, and for a moment Delia looked as though she had been slapped. But when Sebastian came up to ask what she wanted to drink, her smile was brilliant as she greeted him and asked for her usual Bacardi and Coke.

She scintillated throughout the evening, but Max seemed riveted to Felicia's side, and Roxanne could have shaken him. The last thing Delia needed was a lesson in jealousy, which Max seemed determined to give her. She looked for Neal after they had eaten, wondering if he minded his wife being monopolised by another man. Deep in conversation with Sebastian and Roxanne's father, he didn't seem to be bothered at all.

She was making coffee when Delia came into the kitchen, brightly offering help. Roxanne could have managed, but she accepted with every appearance of gratitude. Delia set out cups and saucers with a will, but when she said, 'Lovely party, Roxanne,' Roxanne could bear it no longer.

'I know it's a perfectly ghastly party for you, Delia,' she said, 'and I'm sorry. I'd hoped that Max might have got over trying to punish you by now. I'm sure he doesn't really give a damn about Felicia, or any other woman.'

'Are you? She certainly seems to have bowled him over.'

'He's putting on an act for your benefit——'

'Some act! He's loving it—lapping it up—and you know it. She's gorgeous, isn't she? And she knows exactly how to wrap a man around her little finger, too. More than I ever did!'

'I don't think she's really like that——'

'Don't you?' Delia laughed shortly. 'Sorry if she's a friend of yours, Roxanne. But she's a collector, a scalp-hunter. It takes one to know one, and she might be more subtle than I ever was, but believe me, she's just the same under that expensive, ladylike veneer of hers.'

'I think you're prejudiced,' Roxanne said, not wanting to believe this analysis of Felicia's character, but finding herself all too easily able to accept it.

'I suppose I am,' Delia admitted. 'But I'm also right.

I want to scratch her eyes out.'

'Because of Max?'

'Yes, damn him—because of Max.' Delia wiped a tear away from her cheek and said, 'Don't worry, I won't do it. I'd hate to spoil your party—and I'm trying to learn to be a lady.'

Her gamine, self-deprecating grin flashed, and Roxanne laughed.

A masculine voice said, 'What's the joke?'

Max had pushed open the door, and was leaning his shoulder against the jamb.

Delia dropped a cup, swore under her breath, and picked it up, saying, 'It's okay, Roxanne. No damage.'

'What's the joke?' asked Max again, coming into the room and standing a few feet away from Delia.

Defiantly, she said, 'Roxanne was laughing because I said I'm trying to learn to be a lady.'

Max smiled himself, as he studied her. Then he said softly, 'Don't try too hard. I reckon you're one heck of a lady as you are.'

She looked startled and then wary. 'What do you mean?' she asked him.

'I'll explain on the way home.'

'I'm going home with the Sherwoods.'

'You're going home with me. The Sherwoods have to leave soon, to let their sitter go home, and the party isn't nearly over yet.'

'You mean you can't bear to tear yourself away from *Mrs* Osborne? I'm surprised her husband doesn't object to the way you've been peering down her neckline all night!'

Max grinned. 'What's the matter, darling? Jealous?'

'Huh!' Delia tossed her head. 'Of course I'm not jealous! I just think that if you're going to call *me* names for getting on with guys, you ought to—to keep your own house in order. She *is* a married woman, you know.'

'Sure she is. And if I was her husband, I'd have put her over my knee before now.'

'Oh! You male chauvinist *pig*!'

Roxanne, an interested spectator until now, said approvingly, 'Good for you, Delia!' and then dived for the electric jug as it spurted boiling water on to the bench.

Mopping up, she said, 'Either make yourself useful or get out, Max. You can carry some of those cups through as you go.'

When the three of them returned to the lounge, Felicia was talking to Sebastian, and Roxanne looked at them rather carefully. Felicia was seated in a graceful pose in a deep chair, her body provocatively inclined towards Sebastian, who sat on the arm of the chair, with his hand resting on the back. Felicia was smiling, and once raised her hand towards him, but let it drop before it touched him in any way.

Roxanne passed coffee, aided by Delia, and when the Sherwoods rose reluctantly and said they had to go, she flashed a glance at Delia.

'Sorry to drag you away, Delia,' said Grace.

'You're not,' Max said clearly. 'I'm giving Delia a lift.'

'Oh, good!' Grace was pleased, and although Delia shot Max a look sparkling with resentment, she remained silent.

The neighbouring couple left soon after the Sherwoods, and Roxanne's parents followed not long afterwards. The rest lingered for a while, and Neal at last took a seat beside his wife and draped a careless arm about her shoulders, while he talked to Sebastian and Max. Felicia had accepted a last drink from Sebastian and sat with it in her hand, her eyes going from one man to another, something oddly catlike in the way she looked at them. Once her gaze shifted from Max to Delia, and then back to Max again, and

Roxanne thought she saw a hint of anger in the violet depths. Max merely smiled, in his usual cynical fashion, and Felicia jerked her gaze away and, downing the rest of her drink in one gulp, said, 'Neal, isn't it time we were going?'

'Just waiting for you to finish your drink, darling,' he said, getting to his feet.

Max's hand encircled Delia's slender wrist, and he pulled her from her chair. 'Time we were on our way, too,' he said, ignoring her effort to free herself. Delia shrugged and gave up, her reddened mouth in a sulky pout.

'You didn't bring a jacket, did you?' Roxanne asked.

Delia said no, and Sebastian was already holding the light wrap that Felicia had thrown carelessly over the back of one of the chairs. She smiled over her shoulder as he put it on for her, and he returned it with a rather tight, oddly sardonic smile of his own.

The Osbornes went first, and Max put Delia into his low, sporty car while Roxanne hovered with Sebastian at the edge of the drive. 'Thanks for the dinner,' said Max, kissing Roxanne's cheek. She plucked at his sleeve as he straightened, and said in an urgent undervoice, 'Max!'

'Don't worry!' he whispered, his fingers touching her arm. 'I know—she's as nervous as a kitten, and spitting with it. At least I've got her talking to me again, even if it's only to abuse me! Thanks again, Roxanne.'

She watched them drive off, her fingers crossed, and Sebastian noticed and picked up her hands to straighten them. 'I think Max knows exactly what he's about,' he said. 'Delia will lead him a dance, but she'll give in, in the end.'

'Well, I hope she doesn't give in too easily,' said Roxanne with a hint of tartness, as they went back into the house. 'It seems to me he's a mite over-confident.'

Sebastian laughed. 'What happened in the kitchen? Max muttered something about "female solidarity" when he came out. Did you and Delia gang up on him?'

'Nothing he couldn't cope with,' she said dryly. 'Delia called him a male chauvinist pig, and I agreed with her.'

'Why, was he having another go at her?'

'Actually, he was talking about Felicia. And I don't think I'll tell you what he said. She's a friend of yours, after all.'

She picked up some glasses and cups and put them on a tray. Sebastian undid his tie and pulled it off, then opened the top buttons of his shirt. 'Neal's my friend,' he said. 'Felicia happens to be his wife.'

Roxanne said, 'Does that mean you don't like her?'

'No.' He turned from her, picking up an ashtray and taking it into the kitchen, walking away.

She followed slowly with the tray, and piled the glasses into the sink. Trying to sound casual, she said, '*Do* you like her?'

He gave a strange little laugh. 'Do you know, I've never thought about it. I was——'

He stopped so abruptly that she turned to look at him. 'You were—what?'

His eyes looked past her, brilliant and distant. 'Nothing,' he said shrugging. 'Why the inquisition?'

'It isn't an inquisition. I'm curious about your friends. Doesn't Neal mind when his wife spends an entire evening making a dead set at another man?'

'I think Max wasn't exactly waiting about.'

'Well, she certainly played up to him. Is she always like that?'

'Felicia is one of those rare women who are all things to all men. Are you sitting in judgment?'

'No. I'd be curious to know what she is to *you*, though.'

It was a shot at random, because she sensed that he was tense about Felicia, that under the surface of his light fencing, there ran a deeper undercurrent.

Sebastian's eyes narrowed, and he straightened and moved away from the table. His hands took her face and tilted it up. 'She's my friend's wife,' he said. 'Who's been talking?'

'Is there anything to talk about?' she asked him, suddenly wondering if there was.

His hands tightened, and his face took on a cruel cast. 'I said, *who*?'

'No one!' Her fingers closed on his wrists, trying to drag them away from her. 'Stop it, Sebastian! You're hurting!'

His hands left her face, but only to grip her by the shoulders, digging into the flesh of her upper arms. 'Someone's been stirring up trouble, haven't they?' he demanded. 'Was Max throwing out hints? It would be like him to put together two and two and come up with five—or six.'

'It wasn't Max,' she said. 'Call it intuition. What happened, Sebastian? Did you have an affair with Felicia?'

'No,' he said coldly, 'I didn't. So button up your suspicious little mind, my darling wife. You're barking up the wrong tree.'

He pulled her close and kissed her, with a residue of angry impatience. Roxanne's mind ran in circles, sure that there was something he was not telling her, bothered by his temper and his evasions.

She moved her mouth from his, and his lips went to the curve of her shoulder. 'Come to bed,' he muttered.

'No.' She tried to pull out of his embrace, but he swung her into his arms, and took her into the darkened bedroom.

She kept saying no as he threw her down on the bed and joined her there, and as he shrugged out of his shirt she placed her hands against his chest, protesting until he kissed her into silence. She fought as he slid down the straps of her dress and tugged at the zipper, but stopped, panting with frustration and exertion, when he said, 'It's a pretty dress. It would be a shame to tear it.'

'You *wouldn't*!' she hissed in the darkness. And Sebastian said, with grim purpose that left her in no doubt, 'Wouldn't I?'

He peeled the dress from her body and tossed it to the floor. Roxanne aimed a slap at him, and his fingers closed on her wrist and forced it down. She knew he was stronger, but she struggled for her pride's sake, while his hands held her still and his mouth explored her skin, until she felt a spiralling excitement, and her limbs seemed to grow weak with desire.

She moaned and her head moved from side to side, and suddenly he let go her imprisoned wrists and thrust his hands into her hair, holding her so that he could see the white blur of her face, and the brilliant darkness of her eyes.

'I don't go in for rape,' he said. 'Tell me you don't want this, and I'll stop——'

Irrationally, she wished he had not asked her. She didn't want him to stop now. And she didn't want him to know how strong her own desire was. She lay still under him, her breathing gasping and uneven, and her body tense with anticipation.

'Well?' Sebastian said softly.

'Damn you!' she whispered, half sobbing, with a mixture of anger and laughter. She put her arms up and linked them about his neck, and he lowered his body to hers and kissed her into a mindless, breathless, frenzied wanting, before he finally gave her the satisfaction that she craved, and took from her the ultimate gift of her body that she was longing to bestow.

CHAPTER TEN

THREE days later, Delia came into the shop wearing a diamond solitaire on her left hand that made Grace's eyes widen incredulously.

'Like it?' Delia asked, holding up her hand for Roxanne's inspection.

'It's beautiful! And I'm very happy for you.' Roxanne hugged her and kissed her cheek with genuine warmth. 'When is the wedding?'

'Very soon! Max didn't want to wait at all—he says he wants a ball and chain on me—but I'd hate people to think it's a shotgun job, so we're waiting for a month.'

Grace squeaked, 'Max? Max *Ansell*?'

Roxanne shot her a warning look, and Delia said, 'That's right.'

Grace stammered, 'Oh. W-well, how—how lovely!'

After Delia had danced out, Grace said again, in stunned accents, 'Max Ansell!'

'It's been on the cards for some time, actually,' Roxanne told her. 'He's a lucky man.'

Grace looked doubtful.

Sebastian's reaction was less surprised, of course. Roxanne told him as he drove them home after work. He was spending a lot of time at the Challis/Renner factory, which it now was, and except on the days he had to be in Auckland they drove home together, although he had given her a car of her own.

His eyes on the road ahead of them, where it wound into a clay cutting overhung with red-tinted ladder ferns and the silver-leaved umbrellas of the taller tree ferns, he grinned and said, 'Good for Delia.'

A little nettled, Roxanne said, 'It wasn't entirely her idea, you know.'

'I don't suppose it was. But she knew when to stop running, didn't she? Probably as soon as she realised that Max had marriage in mind, I'd say.'

She turned on him indignantly, saw the faint crease of humour at the corner of his mouth, and realised she was being teased.

'Actually,' she said, 'we women are not all pantingly awaiting the day when some man deigns to offer us a wedding ring! Marriage is no longer the be-all and end-all of a woman's existence. Some of us prefer to dispense with it altogether.'

'Including you?' he said softly, and the humour had entirely disappeared from his expression.

'I didn't say that.'

'You're very good at not saying things, Roxanne.'

'What do you mean?'

'Never mind. We've been invited to spend the day with Neal and Felicia on Saturday, at their bach.'

'That will be nice,' she said formally.

'Do you like fishing?'

'Not specially. Are we going fishing?'

'Neal will no doubt want to take me out in his boat. Felicia isn't keen, either, so you two girls can keep each other company while we try our luck on the wide blue sea.'

It sounded like a perfect day for the men, Roxanne thought sourly. She was tempted to suggest he go alone, but not wanting to be the sort of wife who created strains in her husband's friendships, she kept silent.

In the event, Felicia greeted her charmingly, with every appearance of pleasure. 'We'll have a perfectly lazy day,' she said gaily. 'It's cool for swimming, but I know a spot that's always warm if there's a bit of sun, and we can sunbathe and gossip.'

They had lunch first, soup followed by cold meat and salad, and served with white wine. Then the two women saw the men off in the small boat with an outboard motor attached to the stern, and turned back to the beach house.

They washed the dishes first, then Felicia produced a large, light rug and a couple of beach towels, and packed some fruit and a bottle of wine into a basket. 'Got your bikini?' she asked Roxanne, who nodded. She was wearing it under the scarlet linen shift. Felicia had a light muslin caftan on, her own minuscule black bikini showing through its folds.

'Come on, then,' she said. 'Oh—glasses!' She stopped to place two long-stemmed glasses into the basket. 'Well, I don't see why we shouldn't,' she said, catching Roxanne's glance. 'The men took a half dozen cans of beer with them.'

Roxanne smiled. In this mood, Felicia was rather likeable. Roxanne began to hope that they might become friends, after all.

The secluded spot on the beach was everything that Felicia had promised. Bounded by an outcrop of rocks and a huge pohutukawa whose ancient roots dug into the sand, sagging branches bowed almost into the water, the little half-moon bay was sheltered from most breezes, and a perfect spot for winter sunbathing. They stripped to their bikinis, and Roxanne saw that already Felicia had acquired a light, pretty tan that enhanced her luscious figure.

They used some suntan lotion and settled on the rug. Felicia had huge sunglasses to cover her eyes, but Roxanne lay with its warmth beating against her closed lids. She was almost asleep when Felicia said, 'Have some wine?'

She would have said no, thanks, but when she opened her eyes the other woman was kneeling at her side, holding two brimming glasses.

Roxanne sat up, hunching her knees in front of her, and took one of the glasses. The wine was still cool, and refreshing. Felicia drank hers with almost sensual enjoyment, tipping back her head so that her throat was elongated, the golden skin taut and smooth. Her eyes were closed, and when she lowered the now half-emptied glass, the tip of her tongue licked slowly over her moistened lips. 'Mm,' she murmured, opening her extraordinary violet eyes. 'Delicious, isn't it?'

She leaned back, one knee raised, and held the glass up in front of her so that the sun sparkled through it. 'You look like a pagan goddess,' Roxanne told her involuntarily.

Felicia glanced at her in pleased surprise, her red lips curved in a smile. She looked exquisitely beautiful and decidedly sexy, and it crossed Roxanne's mind that men must find her very nearly irresistible.

Felicia drained her glass, and said, 'We should finish it while it's cool, really. Have another.'

Roxanne shook her head, holding up her own glass as evidence that it was three quarters full still.

'Slowcoach,' Felicia said goodhumouredly, and poured herself another, leaning over to top up Roxanne's glass in spite of her protest. 'Be a devil,' she advised gaily. 'Sebastian isn't here to stop you.'

'What makes you think he'd stop me?' Roxanne asked curiously.

'Sebastian doesn't approve of ladies drinking—haven't you found that out? Well, make that *excessive* drinking, I suppose. He's very disapproving if one gets a little tipsy.'

'I know.' Roxanne could have bitten out her tongue as she said it, recalling the incident in Rotorua, but Felicia smiled delightedly and said,

'So you have found it out! Was he terribly angry?'

Roxanne shook her head, flushing, and sipped at her wine.

Felicia grimaced. 'Oh, he was terribly controlled, was he? You poor dear. I expect that was even worse.'

Roxanne contrived a light laugh. 'You know him very well.'

There was a strange little silence, and Roxanne looked up to find Felicia regarding her fixedly. Then she laughed, too, but it sounded strained and artificial. 'Of course,' she said. 'Neal and I have known him for a long time.'

She had dragged in her husband's name deliberately, Roxanne knew. The atmosphere had changed, subtly. Felicia finished the wine in her glass, and replaced the bottle in the basket. She lay down on her stomach and unhooked the strap of her bikini top, her face turned away from Roxanne.

Roxanne sipped at her wine reflectively, her eyes on the blue sheet of the sea stretching to the horizon, with its curling edge of white breakers. Gulls flung themselves screaming into the air from the rocks, and a couple of white-fronted terns picked their way gracefully along the water's edge. Felicia seemed to be dozing, and after a while Roxanne lay down and tried to do the same. But she was relieved rather than anything when dark clouds began to shadow the sun and Felicia sat up in the sudden ominous chill and shivered, saying, 'Heavens! It looks as though we're in for a wetting. We'd better pack up and go.'

They made it to the house just before the rain came pelting down, and Felicia laughed and pulled out the bottle of wine, surveyed what was left and poured for both of them. 'Might as well,' she said. 'The men will be here soon, I should think, and there's not enough left for them.'

'Will they be all right?' Roxanne took her glass over to the long window facing the sea, and tried to glimpse the water through the curtain of the rain.

'Oh, they'll be fine, don't worry.'

When they came in they were drenched, but apparently in good spirits, indulging in some masculine teasing of each other, and more interested in displaying the three quite respectable fish they had caught before the rain came down than in changing their sodden clothes for dry ones.

After a few minutes, when they had been standing in the kitchen dripping all over the floor and exchanging mild insults for what she evidently considered long enough, Felicia said rather sharply, 'Well, as a wife of many years, I'm accustomed to being ignored, but your new bride was anxious about you, Sebastian.'

The men's grins faded. Neal looked sheepish, and said something heavily gallant to Felicia about her being the last woman in the world a man could ignore, while Sebastian looked across at Roxanne with a lifted eyebrow and a questioning look in his dark eyes.

Roxanne looked away, and Neal took Sebastian into the bedroom to find a change of clothes for them both.

It wasn't until they were back home in their own bedroom at the end of the day that Sebastian asked Roxanne, '*Were* you worried about me today?'

'I expect Felicia was expressing her own anxiety, in a roundabout way,' she answered. 'I wasn't hysterical.'

He slanted a glance at her and said, 'No, you wouldn't be. Were you calculating the chances that you were free of me, after all?'

It was like a slap in the face. After a moment she said shakenly, 'That's a horrible thing to say.'

'Is it? I apologise. As you've reminded me on several occasions, you were a very reluctant bride.'

Roxanne looked away from him. She was standing by the dressing table, her fingers on the carved featherbox, Sebastian's first present to her. 'That doesn't mean I would wish you dead,' she said. 'I don't regret our bargain, Sebastian.'

And Sebastian said, 'I do. I don't think I've ever regretted anything so much in all my life.'

She swung round to look at him, but he was leaving the room, roughly pulling off the shirt he had borrowed from Neal, making his way to the bathroom.

He was a long time coming back, and when he did, his face wore a remote expression and his voice was clipped as he told her he was going to Auckland next day and would be away for the entire week.

'It's a sudden decision, isn't it?' she asked.

'No. I just haven't remembered to tell you about it before, that's all.'

'I see.'

'Will you be all right here, alone?'

'Yes. I'm not nervous, and if I get lonely, I'm sure Mum and Dad wouldn't mind putting me up for a few nights.'

Sebastian got into bed and picked up a book, and Roxanne went along to the bathroom, her thoughts in confusion. When she got back, he had switched off his bedside light and seemed to be sleeping. She suspected he wasn't, really, but obviously he didn't want to talk, to explain what he had meant by that ambiguous remark about regretting their bargain. And she knew from experience that it was no use nagging him for an answer he was determined not to give.

He left quite early in the morning, saying he would go to the flat and catch up on some paperwork, ready for Monday. 'I've been so busy here with the amalgamation, I've neglected the other branches,' he said. 'Your father can manage alone this week.'

'I expect he can,' she said mechanically. 'Has the merger been a financial loss for you, Sebastian?'

'It's cost money, so far,' he said. 'But in the long run it will come right.'

'I'm—grateful,' she said gropingly, 'for what it's

done for my family.'

He inclined his head rather ironically, and said, 'Yes, I know you are. You've shown your gratitude quite convincingly, don't think I don't appreciate that.'

She knew he had misunderstood what she was trying to say, and her cheeks flamed in mute distress.

He laughed, a short, rather cruel, harsh sound, and kissed her quickly on the mouth, and then was gone, the sound of his car receding down the drive and being swallowed in the roar of the waves on the beach. The water was high this morning, under a grey sky. In the aftermath of a storm at sea, the breakers were laden with long strands of brown kelp and bobbing driftwood which they deposited along the sand, so that by the afternoon it was littered with bundles of tangled seaweed and piles of whitened, twisted wood.

And the afternoon brought Felicia, white-faced and with glittering eyes looking black in the blue hollows that surrounded them, wearing a wide-collared blouse and black fitting corduroy pants that were muddied about the hems, and carrying an airline bag.

'Can I come in?' she asked, when Roxanne opened the door to her knock. She sat down on the sofa and took a small make-up sachet from the bag she had placed on the floor, and found a mirror. 'My God!' she grimaced. 'I look awful!'

'I didn't hear a car,' Roxanne said, puzzled. 'Is Neal with you?'

'I didn't come in the car,' said Felicia. 'Well—I started out in the car, but I forgot to check the petrol gauge, and when I ran out there wasn't an open garage within miles—Sunday, you know. So I hitch-hiked this far. I thought Sebastian might give me a lift to Auckland. He said something yesterday about going there this week.'

'He's gone,' said Roxanne.

'Gone!' Felicia seemed about to cry, her face working strangely. 'The story of my life,' she said bitterly. 'Oh, God! What the *hell* am I going to do now?'

'What's happened?' Roxanne asked, uneasy and concerned. 'Where's Neal?'

'Neal?' The other woman laughed without humour. 'Probably out in his bloody boat, I suppose. Gone *fishing*! He wasn't there when I got up this morning, and I thought, this is it. I've had enough. And I left him. That's what I've done. I've left my husband.'

Roxanne sat in stunned silence, not knowing what to say. Felicia looked defiant and pleased with herself, and she slipped the mirror back into the bag, then said, in something like her normal tones, 'Can I have a drink, Roxanne? I need something to steady my nerves.'

'Yes, of course. What would you like? I'll make some coffee or tea, shall I?'

'Well, later, perhaps. Just now—have you any vodka or gin?'

There was a little of both, so Roxanne brought them out, and a glass, and let Felicia pour what she wanted.

'I could drive you to Auckland,' she offered rather reluctantly, 'if you're sure that's what you want. But don't you think you should let Neal know where you are? If he finds the car, he might be worried.'

'All he'll be worried about is his precious car!' Felicia downed a glass of gin, and reached for the bottle again.

'I'm sure that isn't true,' Roxanne said firmly.

'Are you? My dear girl, you know nothing about it. It's been Neal and me and Sebastian for years—and now *you* come along and spoil it all, and you think you can tell me about my marriage!' Felicia sounded suddenly vicious.

Roxanne went white. 'I didn't mean to tell you anything about your marriage,' she said. 'I just think that Neal will be concerned about you if he doesn't know where you are. But perhaps you might tell me how I've spoiled anything for you?'

Felicia looked almost guilty. 'Forget it,' she said, and emptied her glass. 'Put this away,' she added, pushing the bottle towards Roxanne. 'It's a bad habit, drinking in the daytime. I don't, usually.'

Roxanne put the bottle away, and placed the vodka beside it in the cupboard. She made coffee without asking Felicia if it was wanted, and took two cups into the lounge.

Felicia was standing in the middle of the room, looking about her.

'This is nice,' she said. 'You're a very lucky girl.'

Roxanne put the two cups down on the low table in the centre of the room, and straightened. 'Why do you say it like that?' she asked, because there had been bitterness in Felicia's face.

'You don't know, do you?' said Felicia, her voice high and somehow excited. 'You don't know a damn thing!'

Her eyes were so bright they looked feverish, and the paleness of her face was accentuated by two small flushed spots on her high cheekbones.

'I think it's time I did, don't you?' Roxanne asked quietly, standing very still. She was tired of hints and suspicions. If Felicia knew something she didn't know, she wanted to hear it. At least she would know where she stood.

'It could have been all mine,' Felicia said jerkily. 'All this——' her eyes roved about the room, covetously. 'If only I'd made up my mind to leave Neal sooner. If only I hadn't been such a coward—such a fool!'

Roxanne remained still, trying to assimilate what the other woman was saying. And Felicia suddenly laughed, an ugly, almost hysterical laugh. 'Sebastian's been in love with me for years,' she said. 'He never looked at another woman—not seriously. But I was busy being a faithful wife. Then one night, at a party, I—let go a bit. And Sebastian—had his hopes raised, I suppose. He asked me to leave Neal and go away with him, and when I wouldn't, he stayed away for a while. Then he came and told me he'd bought this place. Out of the way, very private, and on the way to the bach. I come to the bach alone sometimes, when Neal's busy. It would be easy enough to slip in here, on the way, for a few hours—a night. He had it all worked out. He'd bought us—a love-nest, you see. But I said no. I wouldn't cheat on Neal. I might flirt, but I couldn't contemplate an affair with Neal's best friend. So he came back here, and got engaged to you. Love on the rebound—or simply revenge on me.'

Roxanne was listening to all this, wanting to reject it, but it all fitted, the seclusion of the house, the tension she had sensed between Sebastian and Felicia. And suddenly she recalled other small things that took on a new significance—the sparkling wine and the crystal glasses which Sebastian had produced, even though the house was barely half furnished at the time—the candles that had graced the table on their first night here together, after their foreshortened honeymoon. Had he planned the candlelight and the sparkling wine for Felicia?

'Your coffee's getting cold,' she said.

Felicia cast her a curious glance, and came and sat down to drink the coffee. Tiredly, Roxanne took the other cup and sank into a chair opposite.

'I shouldn't have told you,' said Felicia. Promise you won't let Sebastian know I told you. He'd kill me.' She gulped at her coffee, shivered, and said, 'You mustn't mind. I'll go away. I won't see him again. I'm sorry.'

Roxanne felt sick. Unable to finish her coffee, she replaced the cup on the table.

'When would you like to leave?' she asked.

'Soon—please. I'll go and stay with a friend—she's

divorced, she'll understand. But first I'd like to pick up some clothes, and—I'd rather reach the house before Neal gets there. I don't want to see him.'

Roxanne drove her to Auckland, unable to shake off the feeling that she was doing something wrong, but reminding herself that Felicia was a grown woman, and knew what she wanted—or if she didn't, it certainly wasn't Roxanne's place to point it out. She did half-heartedly offer a bed for the night, which Felicia turned down. And surely it was better to give her a lift than to let her hitch-hike the rest of the way? The dangers of that mode of transport were well known, and Felicia must have been feeling pretty desperate to have resorted to it in the first place.

She waited while Felicia packed some clothes, and then drove her to her friend's place. She promised not to reveal Felicia's whereabouts to Neal and, with her thoughts in turmoil, went to the flat. She had her own key, but she sat in the car for some time before deciding to go in there. Sebastian's car wasn't in the garage, and she was tempted to turn right round and drive home again, not letting him know she had been here at all. But she felt the need to confront him, and besides, a nagging worry about Neal stayed in her mind. Apparently Felicia had left him no message, and surely Sebastian, his oldest friend, was a better person to convey the news that she was safe and well, but had left him, than Roxanne, who scarcely knew him?

His oldest friend, and his wife's would-be lover?

Was that what Sebastian had been? Felicia had said so, and she had been very convincing. But Delia had said Sebastian had spent a weekend with her—and later, speaking of Felicia, Delia had said, 'It takes one to know one. She's a collector, a scalp-hunter.'

Well, maybe she was, but it didn't necessarily make her a liar. And it explained so many things, that story of Felicia's. Sebastian's proposal had surprised her at the time. She hadn't thought, until then, that he was in love with her. If he had proposed out of pique, to revenge himself on Felicia, that explained it. And he had taken Roxanne to meet Felicia and Neal just as soon as he possibly could. To hurt Felicia? To show her that he could do without her?

Roxanne remembered his lovemaking, and told herself it must prove something. And logic said, what? That he could desire one woman while loving another? It wasn't so uncommon, and came easily to men, by all accounts. She remembered his determination to marry her, even though he despised her for deceiving him. And his hard refusal to allow her to make a fool of him. Because he felt that Felicia, having turned him down, would laugh at the failure of his attempt to show her how little he cared?

It seemed all too possible, and Felicia's parting words were no comfort. 'Forgive me,' she had said, 'for taking advantage of you. Sebastian has too, hasn't he? But he's lucky—you're a nice girl. You could make him happy, Roxanne—make him forget me. I'm sure it will turn out for the best, in the end.'

Roxanne wandered about the empty flat, watching the clock and wondering how long Sebastian would be, and fingering the black leather upholstery that Delia had once described so graphically.

She didn't feel like a nice girl, she felt like a wronged woman, it was useless to remind herself that at least Sebastian had told the truth when he denied having had an affair with Felicia. It was the kind of truth that concealed a lie. And that lie was the basis of their marriage. She had believed that at least when he proposed, he had loved her. She had thought, later, that she might rediscover or revive that love, and lately she had begun to believe that she had done it.

Now, it seemed that all that had been self-deception.

Oh, where was he? Why didn't he come home? He was supposed to be catching up on paperwork. At the office? She could phone there, but what would she say? 'I'm at the flat. I want to talk to you.'

Well, she could say that. Her hand hovered over the phone, and then stopped. She didn't want him to have any warning. She didn't want him arriving wary, with his mask in place, ready for anything.

Felicia had said she could make him happy. Well, she wanted to do that. But anger kept getting in the way. She wasn't the sweet, submissive type who was content to take the crumbs left over from her husband's love of another woman. She didn't see herself waiting patiently, lovingly, for him to turn to her for comfort. And when she began to wonder if he had thought of Felicia every time he made love to her, she wanted to scream and throw things, a primitive rage burning inside her until she was shaking with it.

She thought of him buying that house and getting it ready for Felicia, and then of him taking *her* there, and sharing with her the bed he had meant for Felicia, in their quiet, secluded 'love-nest'—she thought of herself as a substitute, because the woman he really wanted was unattainable, or as an anodyne for the pain that Felicia had given him. She tried to see a value in that, in the possibility that he might have used her to assuage the hurt, and perhaps she should have been comforted by that, but she wasn't. She was sickened, because whichever way she looked at it, he had been *using* her, and she couldn't stomach that—that he had looked on her as something for his use, not a person, loving and needing love, but a thing like all the other things he owned.

She had said once that he was buying her, and it had made him angry. Perhaps because it was too close to truth for comfort? But maybe that had salved his conscience, in the end. Maybe he did look on their marriage as a transaction, on herself as a marketable commodity.

And what had he meant when he said that he regretted their bargain? It was after they had spent the day with Neal and Felicia. And it was after that that Felicia had decided to leave Neal. Had Felicia's talk about 'things working out' for Sebastian with Roxanne been just a blind? Supposing she had phoned him at the office, could he be with Felicia now?

'*Good heavens, no!*' she said to herself aloud. Suspicion was making her paranoid. No woman, surely, would inveigle her lover's wife into conveying her to a rendezvous with him! Would she?

It was ludicrous. And yet there was something about Felicia, some quality that made the idea not quite unthinkable.

She was sitting on one of the black leather couches with her forehead resting on one hand, when she heard Sebastian's key in the lock and he came in.

She could have sworn that the leap of light in his eyes when he first saw her was pleasure, but surprise quickly succeeded it, and he said, 'Hello! Anything wrong?'

'I gave Felicia a lift,' she said, trying to sound casual. 'Their car broke down.'

'Bad luck,' he said. 'I take it Neal was with her?'

'No, he—was still back at the bach, I gather.'

'Funny. I thought they were both coming back today. In fact, Neal had better be here tomorrow—I'm counting on having him in on a conference——'

The telephone shrilled, and Sebastian picked up the receiver from the desk in one corner of the room. She heard him say, 'Hello, Neal, I hear you've got car trouble?'

Then he swivelled to look at Roxanne as he listened, and said, 'Actually Roxanne is here—she tells me she gave Felicia a lift. Just a moment.'

He said to Roxanne, 'Where did you drop her, Roxanne? Neal's just arrived back in Auckland and he's worried about her.'

'She's perfectly all right. She called at the house and then went on to a friend's place.'

'Where?'

Roxanne hesitated and shrugged.

'You mean you dropped her at the house, and she said she was going on elsewhere?'

'She's quite all right,' Roxanne repeated. 'Just let Neal know that, Sebastian.'

Sebastian stared at her, then slowly spoke into the receiver. 'Roxanne says she was quite okay, and has gone to a friend's place . . . I don't know, Neal. I'll see if Roxanne remembers anything—and ring you back.' He rang off.

'What's going on?' he demanded. 'If you know where she is, for God's sake why not say so? Neal's going frantic—she left out without so much as a by-your-leave, he found the car abandoned and his wife apparently vanished. There are people out searching for her along the coast.'

'Well, they can stop searching now, she's quite safe.'

'Where?'

She looked at him, stubbornly silent.

'What the hell is the matter with you?' he asked explosively. 'He's her husband, for God's sake! He's got a right to know——'

'She doesn't *want* him to know! I agree she should have left him some word of what she intended—I tried to persuade her to leave him a note, at least. But she's not a child, she's a grown woman, and if she doesn't want to see Neal, if she wants to be somewhere else for a while, it's her business.'

'You don't know anything about the situation,' Sebastian said, exasperation in his voice. 'You're interfering in a marriage.'

'No, I'm not. I've done a favour for another woman, she asked me to respect her confidence, and that's what I'm doing.'

'Feminine solidarity? You don't understand, Roxanne—Felicia's not normal just now——'

'Because she's left her husband? Do you know, that seems perfectly normal to me?'

'I don't know what the hell you mean by that——'

Roxanne laughed, and said, 'No, you wouldn't!' At this moment she felt very militant, at one with all the wronged women of the world, experiencing a definite hostility against the male assumption of rights and prerogatives, and a sudden vast sympathy with liberating doctrines.

'—but it's not important just now,' Sebastian said gratingly. 'You've got to tell me where Felicia is!'

'Well, I'm not going to.'

She stood up, because he was suddenly striding over to the sofa, a black scowl on his face.

He grabbed her shoulders in a painful grip, and she glared hatred at him. 'What are you going to do?' she asked him. 'Beat it out of me?'

'I'm tempted!'

'How typical!' she cried scornfully. 'Is that what Neal will do to Felicia, when he's reclaimed his "property"?'

'Neal's never laid a finger on Felicia, and he never will.' He paused. 'What's she been telling you?'

'Among other things,' she flung at him, out of her hurt and anger, 'that you've been in love with her for years!'

The moment she said it, she knew that it was true. He went white, and then a wash of dark colour came up under his tan, and he let her go.

'What else?' he asked, with deadly quiet.

This, too, Felicia had asked her not to tell, but she hadn't promised, and although she had not meant to do it like this, in a passion of fury, she knew that to keep silent would be unfair, to Sebastian and to their marriage. She had to give him the chance to deny it, if he could. But he wasn't denying it, and it was tearing at something inside her, the fact that he couldn't, that she had seen the truth of his guilt in his face.

'*Go on!*' Sebastian said harshly. 'What else did she tell you?'

Sullenly, because it really didn't seem to matter any more, she said, 'That you wanted her to be your mistress, and she turned you down. You bought the house at the beach with her in mind, because it was close to the Osbornes' bach, and you thought she could meet you there without Neal finding out. And that you married me on the rebound.'

'The bitch,' he said quietly. 'The little bitch.'

'She said you'd kill her if you knew she'd told me.'

'I might. She'd better pray that Neal finds her first.'

Roxanne smiled bitterly. 'She knows you very well, doesn't she? Much better than I ever did.'

'You believed her,' he said, looking at her with eyes that seemed to sear into her soul. 'You believed that farrago of nonsense!'

'Nonsense? Are you telling me there's no truth in it? It's all nonsense, is it?'

'Yes,' he said, just a split second too late, but she had noticed the tell-tale hesitation, and she said with angry contempt, her lip curling over her shut teeth, 'You *liar*!'

'Roxanne!' He reached for her, but she shied away from him, turning her shoulder, not wanting to look at his face, with the flush of guilt on the strong cheekbones, and the frustrated anger in his eyes. 'Don't touch me!' she said fiercely. 'I couldn't bear you to touch me.'

'Roxanne, *listen*!' He touched her arm, and she flung

his hand away from her, retreating from him in apparent disgust. His face taut, he said, 'All right, all right, I won't touch you. Just—listen, will you? It's important that we find Felicia——'

'For Neal, or for you?' she taunted.

'*Shut up!* I'm trying to explain—this is important.'

She closed her lips and tilted her chin, pointedly listening. Sebastian took a deep breath and said, 'Felicia has a drinking problem. She won't admit it, and neither will Neal, but he's beginning to realise that she needs help now. He opened up yesterday, a bit, and told me that he's worried about her. You can imagine how worried he is now. He sounded frantic when he spoke to me. Let me phone him back and tell him where she is.'

Roxanne chewed on her lower lip uncertainly. Remembering Felicia's inroads on the wine yesterday, after the wine they had drunk at lunch, and her demand for a drink as soon as she had arrived today, it could well be true. But she had not seemed affected by the alcohol, and she had told Roxanne to put away the remainder, and said she didn't normally drink in the afternoon . . .

'I've only your word for it,' she said stubbornly.

'I see. And you don't think much of my word at the moment.'

She said nothing to that, and Sebastian finally said, 'Would you believe Neal, if he told you himself?'

'I might. And it might not make any difference.'

He looked angry, but he was controlling it. 'He won't want to leave the house,' he said. 'In case she comes back. I'll take you round to see him.'

Neal flung the door open when they rang the bell, and fell back with such patent disappointment when he saw them that Roxanne's numbed feelings ached slightly in sympathy.

He hardly waited for them to get into the house before he said to Roxanne, 'Sebastian said she was all right when you left her.'

'Quite all right,' Roxanne assured him.

'Well, that's a relief.' He paused and said, 'Was she quite—normal?'

'She was quite sober,' Roxanne said.

Neal flushed deeply and looked at Sebastian.

Sebastian said carefully, 'Roxanne doesn't believe that Felicia has a drinking problem.'

'Well, she has,' Neal said tiredly. 'I've been denying it to myself for years, but I finally faced up to it last night. She went on a binge, nothing could stop her. She was finding bottles all over the bach—it's only a small house, for God's sake—I had no idea she had so much grog stashed away in the place. It's one of the classic signs, isn't it, when a person hides it? I tried to reason, I told her I'd get her to a doctor, some kind of clinic. She went for me—I'd never have believed it. When she finally passed out, I thought she'd sleep the clock round. This morning I went for an early walk, trying to clear my own head, think things through. And when I got back she'd taken the car and gone. When I found the car up against a tree——'

Roxanne made a startled exclamation, and Neal stopped and looked at her. 'She told me the car ran out of petrol,' she explained.

'I suppose she didn't want to admit that she'd pranged it because she couldn't see straight.' He was sitting on the sofa now, and Sebastian had pushed Roxanne into a chair. 'I was scared stiff that she was still stoned out of her mind, and that she might have done something—I don't know—she could have wandered over a cliff, decided to swim—anything. I've been nearly out of my mind. And then I thought, maybe she was home, and she's been here, and gone. Where, Roxanne?'

'She didn't want me to tell you,' Roxanne said.

'But she told *you*?'

'I took her there.'

His eyes full of hope, he said, 'Roxanne, I understand Felicia. She needs me. I've failed her in lots of ways. She needs excitement, and I'm not exciting. I like a quiet life, and when she's sparking and full of fight, I tend to go off and leave her to it until she's over her temper. She hates that, she'd rather get it out of her system and clear the air, but I'm no fighter, I never have been. She wants lots of attention, and sometimes I fail her there, too. I'm busy, I can't always be dancing attendance on her—and she likes the things I can buy for her, because my job brings in pretty good money, and that takes a lot of time. Sometimes she looks for attention from other men. Last night—last night I discovered that she thinks I don't love her, because I don't fly into a jealous rage when she attracts other men. I just thought, it keeps her happy, it's harmless, why not? I love her—only sometimes I find it hard to show her that I love her, in *her* way, in ways that mean something to her. I want a chance to do that. Roxanne, she likes excitement, but she needs stability, and I'm her stability. She needs me now like she never has before, and I'm willing to accept her needs now, where before I'm afraid I tried to deny them. I could *help* her. She knew I'd ask you where she'd gone. She knew. She made sure that you could lead me to her.'

Roxanne recognised the truth. But she hesitated, and Neal said, 'I'll only talk to her, and if she tells me to go away, I will, I swear. I'll never go near her again unless she asks me. Please, Roxanne.'

'I remember the address,' she said, and told him.

Neal passed a hand over his eyes. 'Thank you,' he said. 'I'll go right away—please excuse me.'

Sebastian said for both of them, 'Yes. Good luck.'

Neal gave them a pale smile, and they all left the house together.

His car had swung out of the drive and taken off before Sebastian had turned the key in the ignition. Roxanne sat with a crease between her brows, worrying at her lower lip, and Sebastian said crisply, 'You did the right thing. He understands her. He's the only one who can help now, and if she's got any sense, she'll accept it.'

Roxanne hoped that Felicia would. Neal loved her, and it seemed it was the thought of treatment for her problem that had panicked her into running from him. She was suddenly sure that Neal would win out in the end.

CHAPTER ELEVEN

BACK at the flat, Roxanne murmured something about returning to Waimiro and Sebastian said forcefully, 'You're going nowhere tonight. It's too late, and we have things to talk about.'

'I *have* driven in the dark before,' she said tartly. 'And I've a shop to open tomorrow.'

He took her arm and hauled her with him along the path, up the steps and into the lounge. 'Damn the shop,' he said, as he closed the door behind him. 'It can wait.'

She rubbed her arm pointedly, where he had held her and, watching, he said, 'You'll be lucky if that's the only bruise you escape with.'

'Brute!'

'Yes, aren't I? Do you think you can stop spitting at me long enough to listen to some explanations?'

'Had time to think up a good story, have you?'

'For God's sake, cool it, Roxanne! I realise you've had a hell of a day, but I'm feeling pretty brutal myself, as you've noticed. I'm trying to look at it from your angle, but my greatest desire at the moment is to shake you senseless!'

The violence in his tone made her swallow her angry retort, but resentment set her mouth in a stubborn line and made her eyes darken as she sat down on the very edge of the black leather.

Sebastian still stood, his hands thrust into his pockets. He took a long, jagged breath and said, 'Look, you know I lied this afternoon. It was stupid, and I realise it's going to make it that much more difficult for you to accept that what I'm telling you now is the truth, absolutely. The fact is, this afternoon it all seemed so—complicated, with you all steamed up and hating me, and Neal waiting for word of Felicia. And when I realised what a tale she'd been spinning you, it seemed simpler and—as I thought—less hurtful to you, to deny the whole thing.'

'Is that your excuse? That you didn't want to hurt me?'

'It isn't an excuse. It's the truth.'

'So you keep saying. But the truth seems to keep changing, doesn't it?'

'Maybe it does, depending on who's telling it. You must have have heard Felicia out, is it too much to ask you to do the same for me?'

'She was very convincing.'

Sebastian sighed. 'Yes, I daresay she was. Her alcoholic fantasies are probably very real to her.'

'You mean, she hallucinated the whole thing?'

'No. It would be tempting to say so, but no. There was a grain of truth in it. When I first saw Felicia, she knocked me for six, and it took me a long time to get over it. I told you once, I'd never thought about whether I like her or not. I fell too hard for that.'

'Love at first sight?' Roxanne asked in a brittle voice, jealousy twisting inside her.

'If it was love, yes. I knew there was nothing to be done about it, she was Neal's wife and, now that I look back, I guess that was part of her attraction. She was unattainable, and I was too busy to engage in a serious pursuit of any woman. With Felicia, I didn't have to bother. She was just—there. I thought it was my secret, until one day I woke up to the fact that she knew, and probably Neal knew. It didn't seem to matter. I suppose, in a way, the situation appealed to the romantic in all of us. Neal was my best friend, he knew I wouldn't step out of line with his wife. Felicia—liked having me on a string. That gave me a jolt when

I realised it. That was when I began to fall out of love, I think, when I discovered just how much she enjoyed it. And Neal was right about her—she found a sense of excitement, of sorts, in playing with my emotions. Neal knew only the half of it, of course, but what he did know didn't bother him, as long as Felicia was happy. I was the one who was—miserable. I backed off, but it was difficult to avoid them altogether. Neal is tied up with the business side of my life, and I couldn't take that from him, he'd done nothing to deserve it and he makes a good deal of his money from Renners. And he didn't want to cut the social connection. So I went on seeing them both. Felicia saw me cooling towards her, though, and she didn't like that. Once, at a barbecue party, she and I found ourselves alone—perhaps she engineered it, I don't know. She teased me and goaded me, and—maybe I'm making excuses, but it seems to me she wanted me to kiss her. And eventually I did . . . rather roughly, I'm afraid. It was the one and only time, and I was horrified afterwards to find that she regarded it as the first step to a full-blooded affair.'

'Horrified?' Roxanne was deliberately sceptical.

With a grim smile Sebastian said, 'Yes. No doubt I sound very Victorian, but the last thing I wanted was an affair with Neal's wife. The temptation was there, I admit, but by this time I was becoming fairly disillusioned with Felicia, and I'd begun to suspect that she was drinking a lot, and wasn't entirely responsible for her actions. The craving for excitement was getting stronger. If she couldn't get it from flirtation and parties, it had to come from extra-marital sex and drinking enough to get high.'

'Are you telling me *you* turned *her* down?'

'Yes. I got myself a place to live out of Auckland, too, so that I wasn't too available, and had a legitimate excuse to see less of them. It didn't seem to be near enough to their beach house to be a problem. I had to be reasonably close to Auckland, and there aren't that many suitable places.'

'So you picked Waimiro.'

'Yes, it seemed ideal. And then I found you. Roxanne——' he came closer to her and said, '—please believe this, if you believe nothing else. When I asked you to marry me, I was in love with you—and no one else. The first time I saw you, the impact was——'

He stopped, making a gesture with his hand, and she asked dryly, 'Like the first time you saw Felicia?'

He didn't answer immediately. Then he said slowly, 'No. Not like that, at all. You were quite different. Not only a contrast in colouring, in style—there was a quality of integrity about you. Something I instinctively trusted.'

Roxanne paled, remembering how she had abused that trust.

'That's why I was so angry,' he said, 'when I found out that you'd meant to cheat me.'

'You felt that you'd been fooled again, by another woman.'

'Something like that. Later, I realised that you'd done it for love—not of me, but for love. And when I got over being jealous and angry because you loved your father and your family enough to compromise your principles, I hoped that one day you'd love me like that, too.'

He sat down beside her, studying her averted face.

'I didn't like you at first,' she told him.

'I know. It piqued me, because from the moment we met I liked you and wanted you. I remember that you came in looking as though you'd just been kissed, and my first thought was, "My God, one day I'd like to make her look like that for me!" Then I realised you were also furious, and I wanted to laugh with sheer relief. "If what's-his-name is out of favour," I thought, "maybe there's a chance for me." I hoped for the passion without the anger.'

In the silence that followed, Roxanne turned to look at him. 'Why?' she whispered. 'Why did you ask me to marry you—why did you make me stick to it?'

'Because I love you. I always have, I always will.'

'You never told me that before.'

'Didn't I? Does it—matter, to you?'

'Of course it matters!' Roxanne said crossly. 'If I'd known that, it wouldn't have mattered about Felicia—about anything!'

Sebastian said softly, with wonder, 'Have I been a fool?'

Filled with an obscure anger and irritation, Roxanne said, '*Yes.*' Her closed fist aimed wildly for his jaw, and she said, 'You might have *told* me!'

He caught her wrist and laughed at her, pulling her close so that any further violence was checked. 'I was waiting for you to tell *me*!' he said. 'I made you marry me, didn't I? I thought that was proof enough that I was completely crazy about you, without giving you the satisfaction of telling you so every day!'

'Well, you said you regretted it!' Roxanne accused.

'I regretted the use of coercion,' he said ruefully. 'It meant that I could never be sure you would have married me without it. And unless you came and said so, how could I know you loved me? You still haven't said it, by the way.'

She looked into his teasing, brilliant eyes and stammered, 'I c-can't—in cold blood.'

Exasperation glittered for a moment, before his eyelids veiled it, and his mouth came down on hers, without warning, without mercy, but with an infinitely tender and passionate persuasion.

Her response was ardent and complete, and when he raised his mouth hers was deeply red and full. He said, 'I won't let you go until I hear it.'

'But I don't want you to let me go,' she whispered back, with a hint of mischief.

His hand tugged at her hair in gentle punishment. 'Witch! I won't let you go, anyway.'

'Sebastian, why did you buy wine and candles?'

'What?' His eyes were dark with impatient puzzlement.

'Wine—and candles—for your house. You had wine and proper glasses when you'd scarcely moved in.'

'I bought them for the celebration—remember? I asked you to share it, to mark my moving into the house. I remember the look you gave me—very disapproving.'

'No, it wasn't. Just—wondering. And the candles? You produced them when we came back from our honeymoon. Awfully opportune.'

'Yes, wasn't it? But actually I bought them on Max's advice. Power cuts, you suspicious little idiot. The lines along that road are notorious for breakages in stormy weather.'

'Power cuts! Of course!'

'Of course!' he echoed dryly. 'Satisfied?'

'Yes. I was just curious.'

'So tell me what I want to hear.' But he didn't give her a chance to speak immediately, his mouth finding hers again, kissing her into breathlessness.

He paused at last, his eyes brilliant on her face, and said, '*Now!*'

'I love you, I love you.' Her fingers touched his hair and his mouth, and she said, 'I wish there was some other way to say it.'

Sebastian's dark eyes smiled into hers. 'But darling, there is!'

He pushed her back against the black leather and began to show her.

Harlequin Plus

ROBERT BROWNING AND ELIZABETH BARRETT

They were the "immortal lovers"—true kindred spirits—of nineteenth-century England. Robert Browning was thirty-two and a rising poet when he met Elizabeth Barrett, six years his senior and a brilliant poet in her own right. It was love at first sight, but two years elapsed before the couple married.

Elizabeth's cruelly possessive father opposed the union, and Elizabeth and Robert finally eloped—an act for which Elizabeth's father never forgave her. The pair went on to spend their blissful married years in Italy, where their poetry became inspired by the beauty of their surroundings and their great love for each other.

Perhaps no words better convey an adoring wife's feelings for her husband than a poem from Elizabeth's *Sonnets from the Portuguese:*

How do I love thee? Let me count the ways.
I love thee to the depth and breadth and height
My soul can reach, when feeling out of sight
For the ends of Being and ideal Grace.
I love thee to the level of every day's
Most quiet need, by sun and candle-light.
I love thee freely, as men strive for Right;
I love thee purely, as they turn from Praise.
I love thee with the passion put to use
In my old griefs, and with my childhood's faith.
I love thee with a love I never seemed to lose
With my lost saints—I love thee with the breath,
Smiles, tears, of all my life—and, if God choose,
I shall but love thee better after death.

Take
these
4
best-selling
novels
FREE
ANNE HAMPSON
gates of steel
ANNE MATHER
sweet revenge
VIOLET WINSPEAR
devil in a silver room
JANET DAILEY
no quarter asked